When the Lilacs Bloom

by

Lavada Dee

When the Lilacs Bloom

Cover Art by *The Wild Rose Press, Inc.*

The Wild Rose Press, Inc.
PO Box 708
Adams Basin, NY 14410-0708
Visit us at www.thewildrosepress.com

Publishing History
First Edition, 2024
Trade Paperback ISBN 978-1-5092-5379-1
Digital ISBN 978-1-5092-5380-7

Published in the United States of America

Rayanne knew she was losing weight and she also knew it wasn't because of her shift. The phone company didn't allow pregnant, even married women, to work, and heaven forbid if they weren't married. As soon as she started to show they would lay her off. Rayanne didn't know what she would do when that happened. Even if her mother was still alive, she wouldn't have been any help and she was almost certain her father didn't want anything to do with her. They had never been close and she didn't have hope of that changing.

"Want a cup of coffee?" Amber asked.

At just the thought Rayanne felt her stomach turn. For her it wasn't morning sickness. It was more like all day sickness. It was no wonder she was losing weight. She turned her head so Amber couldn't see her gulping down bile, but not quick enough.

"Damn," Amber put her cup of coffee down,

"Yeah," Rayanne answered.

Silence filled the room. "What a patch of bad luck. And, it was your first time?" Amber's eyes shown with sympathy.

Rayanne nodded her head.

"Got any ideas on what you're going to do? I could tell Noah and ask him to let Luke know, but I guess it's no secret that I haven't heard a word from him."

Chapter 1

May 1944

Rayanne let out a sigh. It would be nice to curl up with a good book. Nights off were precious, and she'd heard the horror stories about blind dates. Even though she had precious little experience, she listened to the girls at work talking about them and going out with a guy you didn't know sounded scary. Still, it was only for a few hours, and she had promised her roommate, Amber, that she would go out. It was Amber's boyfriend's last night off before deployment to Europe and they needed someone to make it a foursome as he was bringing a friend. With another sigh Rayanne acknowledged that it was too late to back out now, so she better get herself ready.

She ran her hands over the meager clothes in her closet. What to wear? The weather had turned warm for it being early spring in Washington, and Amber had on a sundress. Rayanne had one that she hadn't worn yet, but it was a little to revealing for her to feel comfortable wearing it out with someone she didn't know. Heck, she hadn't even met Amber's boyfriend, let alone his friend.

Amber tapped on the door. "Hurry up, Rayanne. I told Noah we would meet him at the drugstore, and it will take a few minutes to get there."

With a last look in the closet, Rayanne turned back to the bed where she'd laid out a modest little black dress. "This will have to do," she mumbled as she slipped the dress over her head.

Amber was all but pacing the small living room when Rayanne stepped out of the bedroom and announced that she was ready.

"You look great. Noah's friend is going to love that dress. I wish I could sew like you do."

"I wish I could bring my sewing machine from Dad's. Then I could make you some outfits."

Amber was already halfway out the door. Hurrying Rayanne along she said, "We can make room in the apartment for it."

Rayanne shook her head. "We don't have any way to get it here. We would need a truck as we can't very well get it on the bus. Maybe when I settle in better with this job, I'll take some of my days off and go out to Dad's to sew from there."

Rayanne and Amber both worked as switchboard operators at the telephone company in Olympia. She had the graveyard shift while Amber worked swing. Their apartment was tiny, with only one bedroom that barely held a full bed. Having different shifts made it more workable. And, with the house rules of no guests, especially men, they really didn't need a lot of room.

The women hurried down the street. Walking to work at almost midnight, Rayanne had picked up a stride that Amber hadn't yet acquired. "I know I said I didn't want to be late, but we have time," Amber panted.

Just as Rayanne was about to slow down, they rounded the corner and saw two men leaning against a sleek, late model car. Amber pointed to them. "Nice wheels, huh. I wish it were Noah's. He sold his car so he wouldn't have to worry about it while he was overseas."

Rayanne didn't know a lot about cars but this one, she had to admit looked classy. Her gaze drifted toward the men. Both were tall and good looking. The foursome was making sense now that Ambers guy didn't have his own transportation. Rayanne had wondered why Amber would want company on maybe her last date with a guy she hoped would ask her to marry him.

Amber went straight up to one of the men and giving him a kiss on the lips, turned and introduced him to Rayanne as her boyfriend, Noah. The other man smiled and said, "and I'm Luca."

Rayanne felt her face heat up and knew her dreaded blush was in full view. She had to agree with Amber, Noah was good looking but Luke or Luca as he had introduced himself, was movie star handsome. Tall maybe just over six feet he had a dark complexion that even in the darkening evening made his eyes stand out. Rayanne had once seen a display of amber at the state fair and thought it was the prettiest stone she had ever seen. Luke's eyes were the color of the deepest stone in the collection. His gaze held hers.

Amber nudged Noah. "Have you been waiting long?"

"Nah, just got here." Looking over at Rayanne, Noah gave a low whistle.

Amber gave him a light slug on the arm. "Behave, Rayanne is a lady."

"And, a looker. Right, Luke?"

Rayanne felt her face heat up again and knew it was still light enough for the others to see the blush. She ducked her head, but not before she saw Luca give her a wink.

"Do you want to leave the car here?" Amber asked. "It's a safe neighborhood and only a few blocks to downtown."

Noah looked over to Luke. "What do you think?"

"I don't care, but if you want to take a ride later, we probably should drive on downtown."

With that settled, the four climbed into the car. Amber climbed in the back seat with Noah right behind. Luke waited until Rayanne was in the car before closing the door and going around the front to the driver's side.

The bar was overcrowded with a lot of men in uniform. With both the army and air force bases being so close there was never a shortage of men around town, but unlike Amber, Rayanne didn't go out.

The men grabbed a table. "I'll get the first round," Luke said.

Noah nodded. "Beer for me." Looking at Amber he said, "Your usual rum and coke?"

"Yes, and get one for Rayanne too."

Luke looked over to Rayanne. "You okay with that?"

Oh boy, Rayanne wasn't sure. She had thought she'd have just a soda, but what could one real drink hurt.

A couple of hours and a few drinks later, the room didn't seem so loud or smoky and Rayanne had forgotten she couldn't dance. The dance floor, like the bar, was crowded. With the lights low it was made for

4

slow, intimate dancing. Luke pulled back so he was looking down at her. "You're doing great. Are you sure you haven't danced before?"

"We lived out of town and my dad was really strict."

"How long have you been out of school?"

Rayanne knew what he was really asking—*How old are you?* He had looked uncomfortable when Amber introduced her. Laughing she gazed up at him. Gosh, he was so good to look at. Finding her voice, she was surprised at how low it sounded. "I'm twenty-one, Luke."

His gaze met hers until he pulled her closer. She could feel his breath on her hair. He sounded more confident now that she had told him her age. "You smell so damn good," he whispered.

Rayanne felt like she could dance all night. She'd never felt anything like this. Luke was older, and she didn't doubt for a minute a lot more experienced than any guy she had ever met.

The music ended and Luke steered her back to the table. The way she was feeling she was going to switch to soda on the next round, but before Luke could say anything Noah and Amber came up. "Ready to head out to some fresh air?" Noah asked.

Weaving their way out the door, Rayanne breathed in the cool night air. She wasn't ready to call it a night. This was her first "real" date and what a great guy to have it with. Luke was a great dancer, considerate, he had moved them around the crowded floor with experience and ease. Too bad the noise in the bar prevented them from getting to know each other. Her regret made no sense because she would probably never see him after tonight. Still, the feeling lingered.

Luke pulled away from the curb. "You are going to have to tell me where we're going," he interrupted Noah and Amber in the back seat.

"Do you know where Priest Point Park is?"

"No, I am from Percy. We didn't get to Olympia much."

Farm country, that's where Luke grew up. Rayanne should have guessed; he was patient, unhurried, relaxed. "I'll give you directions. It's not very far," Rayanne offered.

A few minutes later Rayanne was thankful the park was so close. The sounds from the backseat were a little embarrassing. To mask them she started a conversation. "So, you're local? Amber said Noah is from Texas. I bet you meet guys from all over the states."

"I did basic training in Texas and for the first year of service was stationed in Colorado, but then got lucky and got sent to McChord. Made my mother happy."

"Do you have a large family?"

"No, and me leaving for overseas is really hard on Mom, though she puts on a brave front."

Luke slowed the car. "What about you. I'm guessing a town girl."

"Guess again. My folks have a house on the west side of town but it's out a ways. It wasn't until two years ago that the bus came within a half mile of it. A half mile isn't much but when you're working the graveyard shift it is scary and when the weather is bad it's a hard way to start a ten-hour day, or night in my case."

Rayanne pointed to a sign. "The park is coming up. I don't know where Noah wants to go after we get inside though."

Luke raised his voice to be heard from the back seat and Noah with a grunt, responded. "Go to the right and then over the road, there's a spot down by the bay that's perfect for…" His voice lowered as he turned back to his partner.

A few minutes later Luke pulled up in a parking area and turned off the car. Noah tapped on the back of Rayanne's seat. "You'll need to get out so we can, sugar."

Still a little tipsy, Rayanne's head had cleared a lot since getting out of the bar. Stepping out of the car, Noah immediately went to the trunk and lifted out a couple of blankets. He threw one to Luke and grabbed a sack of beer. With the bottles clanking he set off down a path with Amber following.

"That didn't take long." Luke turned around in the now quiet parking lot. "It's beautiful out here. Let me get us something to drink and we'll find a spot of our own."

Rayanne didn't want any more to drink but she didn't want to be a party pooper either, so she didn't say anything. Besides she had loved dancing with Luke. He was a strong lead, and in no time, it felt like she had been dancing her whole life. Luke led the way and only went a short distance. Probably a good thing because she doubted Noah and Amber wanted company. Just off the trail there was a secluded level spot that had a peek-a-boo view of the bay.

"Perfect." Luke sighed as he spread the blanket out then reached out for Rayanne's hand to steady her until she sat down. He joined her, still holding her hand in his strong, yet gentle grip.

Rayanne watched his gaze linger on her mouth and then slowly rise until she was looking directly into his beautiful eyes. She barely knew this man and probably shouldn't be here. Yet, somewhere deep inside, she knew he was a good man. An honest one. Still, they'd only just met. A shallow breath escaped her as Luke found her mouth with his. He started out slow and sweet but when her lips parted, he deepened the kiss. Rayanne stopped thinking as her body took over.

Luke's mouth left hers to trail down her neck and without thinking about it she tilted her head to give him better access.

"So sweet," he breathed out.

Rayanne melted closer to Luke's heat.

"This is a bad idea," he whispered.

Without thinking that it was completely out of character, Rayanne took the lead and lowered her mouth to his. In answer she was rewarded by Luke's low moan.

Cool air played over her back as Luke pulled down the zipper of her dress and eased it off her arms. A full moon shone down on them as Luke nudged Rayanne down on her back. His gaze roamed over her body clad only in panties and a bra. "You are gorgeous." He ran his hand down over her hip. His palm felt warm. She loved his hands.

Luke paused, giving her time to respond one way or the other. When she just let her gaze linger on his mouth, he whispered, "If you want to stop, this is the time to say so."

Rayanne closed her eyes. Did she? Should she wait for marriage? What if she never had another chance to do *it* with a guy like Luke? A wave of warmth flooded through her and as if it had a mind of its own, her body decided for her as she reached for his kiss.

Luke's lips followed his hands down her body and his breathing changed, coming faster. Feelings ran through her, stealing her breath. Giving herself up to the man positioned over her, she shifted to give him more access.

"So sweet, so ready," Luke whispered just before a sharp pain radiated through Rayanne. Her body tensed and Luke mumbled, "Damn." The pain subsided almost instantly and Rayanne moved with Luke. She had never felt so alive as her body tightened. She wanted something that seemed just out of reach and when she felt Luke try to pull away, she tightened her legs.

Luke let out his breath and rolled on to his back. Both of them laid silent catching their breaths. Finally, Luke broke the silence. His voice sounded muffled. "I didn't know and I should have." He turned and pulled her against his chest. "You okay?"

"I think so," Rayanne stammered. All of a sudden what had seemed so right felt awkward. "Maybe we should get dressed."

Picking up his clothes, Luke said, "Sure, I'll give you some privacy." He stepped behind a large fir tree.

Rayanne felt a tear escape and roll down her cheek. *Is this what "it" was all about?* She'd heard women whispering about their experiences and it sure seemed it would be more. *Maybe I just drank too much,* she consoled herself as she reached for her clothes.

The night had turned cold as it usually did this time of year and Rayanne couldn't get her zipper up. She shivered and tightened her lips to keep her teeth from chattering.

"Having some trouble?" Luke asked as he walked back to the blanket.

"I can't get this darn zipper up."

"Let me look."

The moon had abandoned them, and Rayanne doubted Luke could see enough to unjam the zipper. She *knew* he couldn't when he put his finger in the underside of the tight-fitting dress and worked the zipper.

"It's stuck on some material. I'm going to have to lower it before I can move it up."

Rayanne sucked in her breath. It seemed to take forever but wasn't much more than a couple of seconds before she felt the zipper moving up her back.

"Thank you." Her voice sounded like she had been running. Trying again, she said, "I hate these long back-zippers. This isn't the first time this has happened. I need to redo it."

"Did you make the dress?"

"I make almost all of my clothes—or did. My sewing machine is out at my dad's so not sure how much I'll be doing now."

"I'm impressed. It looks like it came from an upscale store." Luke picked up the blanket and shook it out. "Let's get back to the car. It will be warmer."

Luke's voice sounded so normal. Like nothing had happened. Rayanne felt relief and told herself to not make so much of what had happened. Other people obviously didn't. Taking his lead like she had done on the dance floor she nodded and followed him back to the parking lot.

The car was warmer but Rayanne felt dumb that she hadn't brought some kind of wrap. She had been born and raised here in the Pacific Northwest and well knew the climate and how cool the nights were. Her discomfort didn't go unnoticed by Luke. Getting out of the car he walked around the front to the passenger door and opened it. Taking off his bomber jacket, he held it out to her.

"I don't want to take your jacket."

"I'm not cold."

He didn't say that he had on more clothes than she did, and she was thankful. The dress choice, with no wrap, had been a mistake even though a small one in comparison to the big one she had just made.

An uncomfortable silence filled the car. Rayanne didn't want to talk about what had happened. Luke's seemingly acceptance of it being normal made her feel naïve, or more exactly, stupid.

Luke shook a cigarette out of the pack on the dashboard. "You smoke?"

"No, I got sick the first time I tried and haven't wanted to since then."

"Probably a good thing. I've quit so many times I've lost count." He stuck the unlit cigarette in his mouth.

"Do you think Noah and Amber will be much longer?"

"Nah, I felt a few sprinkles of rain when I handed the jacket to you. Not even Noah will last long in the rain."

As if on cue, Rayanne heard the two laughing and a few minutes later they were running across the parking lot.

Noah was animated and kept them entertained on the ride back to town. It was really raining by the time they got to the apartment making goodbye's quick.

Rayanne handed the jacket back to Luke.

"You going to be okay?" he asked.

She nodded. "I had a good time dancing. I really didn't know I could do it."

"You're a natural. Get out there and do it more."

Rayanne reached up and kissed him on the cheek. "Be safe." She turned to go in but before she could, Luke put his hand on her arm turning her back to him. "Wait."

He reached into the car and took a paper and pencil out. Writing something on it, he handed it to her. "If-if uh… Hell, if you need to get in touch with me here's my address."

Amber opened the door to the house and hurried in, but Rayanne hesitated and turned to look back. Luke was standing in the rain watching. Was he waiting to make sure they got safely inside? Tears welled in her eyes as she raised her arm and waved. Then slipped inside.

Following Amber up the stairs, both women were aware of the silence in the old house and kept as quiet as possible. It wouldn't do to have their old landlady hear them coming in so late after curfew. Affordable housing was hard to find.

"I hate this place," Amber mumbled.

"It's close to work," Rayanne tried to placate her. It didn't take much to see that Noah hadn't popped the question tonight like Amber was hoping for.

By the time they were in the small apartment with the door closed, tears were streaming down Amber's face. "I hoped. I was so sure."

"I know." Rayanne did know. It was all Amber had

been talking about for weeks. A lot of their co-workers were engaged and even getting married before their men went to the front to fight. But Rayanne had also thought Noah didn't seem like the marrying kind.

As Amber gathered her things and headed for the floors shared bath, Rayanne's thoughts turned to Luke—or *Luca*. He wasn't as rough acting or talking as Noah. More of a gentleman. But did she really know? She looked down at the slip of paper, an old envelop, that he had given her. His name and an address were on it, and he had scrawled, *Take Care Of Yourself,* at the bottom.

Chapter 2

Rayanne felt like she was dragging by the time she got off work. The graveyard shift wasn't one she would have chosen if she'd had a choice. It wasn't that jobs weren't plentiful with so many men in the military. However, the telephone company ones were coveted because of having three shifts and better pay then most jobs outside of the government. Too bad, with the low turnover, she didn't see herself being promoted to one of the other two shifts anytime soon.

She opened the door to the old house with her key. In its day the house had been a large private residence. Now it had been turned into apartments. The one on the bottom floor was large and though she'd only caught glimpses from the foyer, she could tell it was opulent, or had been in its day. The second floor had two small, one-bedroom apartments. One was Amber's and hers. The second one was shared by two other women. There was still evidence of a grand house on this floor. The apartments were rented to women only. Rayanne had never been up to the third floor or attic but from what Amber had told her, the third floor had once held a ballroom.

The foyer was good size with the stairs leading up from it wide and graceful. Now, to Rayanne, as tired as she was, it seemed like the stairs had increased in number.

When she got to the second floor, she quietly, so as not to wake Amber, unlocked the apartment door. Amber's swing shift from four in the afternoon until midnight wasn't a lot better than hers.

She jumped as Amber walked out of the bedroom door. "I thought you'd still be sleeping."

"I had last night off, remember?"

"Oh yeah. Do you have trouble going to bed early?" The two rarely had the same night off. The last one had been two months ago. A night Rayanne knew she would never forget.

"This swing shift is the worst shift ever for my social life."

"I'll trade you," Rayanne said.

"I wish we could. I know I'm never going to see Noah again, stupid me for getting my hopes up. He made it clear in the beginning that he wasn't marriage material." She shrugged like she didn't care, then added, "To get back to our work schedule, this shift is really cramping my style for finding someone else."

Amber started to the kitchen and stopped. "I shouldn't whine. You aren't looking well and it's probably because of working all night. That, and the fact you've been working a lot of overtime."

Rayanne knew she was losing weight and she also knew it wasn't because of her shift. The phone company didn't allow pregnant—even married—women to work. And heaven forbid if they weren't married. As soon as she started to show they would lay her off. Rayanne didn't know what she would do when that happened. She didn't have family to help.

Her mother, even if she was still alive, wouldn't have been any help and Rayanne was almost certain her father didn't want anything to do with her. They had never been close and she didn't have hope of that changing.

"Want a cup of coffee?" Amber asked.

At just the thought Rayanne felt her stomach turn. For her it wasn't morning sickness. It was more like all day sickness. It was no wonder she was losing weight. She turned her head so Amber couldn't see her gulping down bile, but not quick enough.

"Damn." Amber put her cup of coffee down,

"Yeah," Rayanne answered.

Silence filled the room. "What a patch of bad luck. And, it was your first time?" Amber's eyes shone with sympathy.

Rayanne nodded her head.

"Got any ideas on what you're going to do? I could tell Noah and ask him to let Luke know, but I guess it's no secret that I haven't heard a word from him."

Oh no. Just the thought made Rayanne's knees feel weak. She sat down on the worn sofa. "Promise me that if you do hear from Noah, you won't tell him."

"From everything Noah's said, Luke's a good guy. He will help you."

Rayanne felt panic flow over her at the thought. "No, I don't want him to ever know. Trust me. I have strong reasons."

"Then how do you think you're going support yourself and a baby?"

Rayanne didn't have an answer and silence filled the room.

Amber sat down beside Rayanne making the old sofa cushion sag. "I know of a doctor who can help, but he won't do anything after the third month."

"You mean an abortion?" Rayanne's voice was barely above a whisper but sounded louder because of the content.

Amber nodded.

"I can't do that." Rayanne swallowed again to keep what little was in her stomach down.

"It's not too bad."

She knew Amber liked guys and Rayanne shouldn't be surprised at what her friend just revealed, but she was.

Again, silence engulfed the room. Rayanne got up from the sofa and took her coat off, hanging it in the closet by the door. She had to work tonight, but then she had the next night off. And Amber was right about working overtime. She doubted she could keep going the way she was for much longer.

"The bed is ready for you. Why don't I make you some breakfast first?"

At Amber's offer, Rayanne smiled. "You are a good friend. Don't worry about me. I'll think of something. Right now, all I want to do is get some sleep."

"I don't know about a good friend. It's my fault you went out with Luke."

Rayanne gave a little laugh. "That hardly qualifies you as being at fault."

****

Rayanne had made it through another shift. *Now to try to stay up for a few hours.* On her nights off she waited until Amber left for work before going to bed herself. By waiting until after four o'clock in the afternoon she would sleep all night and, until recently, wake up in the morning well rested. To make this happen she purposely didn't sit down much and instead did chores like washing and cleaning the house.

In preparation for today, Rayanne had taken both of their clothes hampers out to the kitchen before she left for work the night before. Amber hated going down to the basement to do the washing but Rayanne didn't mind, so she did it for both of them. She had just started putting the last load through the wringer washing machine when she heard a noise behind her. The basement was dark and the utility sink and washer were back in an even darker corner. Rayanne could understand Amber's dislike of the basement now, as her own heartbeat picked up.

She held her breath, afraid that if she called out her voice would betray her fear. Instead, she gripped the edge of the sink waiting for whoever it was to identify themself.

"I'm sorry if I scared you."

The voice, soft and warm, pulled all Rayanne's breath from her. "Luke?" She turned, still unable to believe it even though he stood right in front of her. He had a golden tan that he didn't have when he'd left. And it looked really good on him… "What are you doing here?"

"Shhh, you don't want your landlady to hear you. Or me. Amber told me how to come through from the backyard. I saw you hang that last batch of clothes on the line and had planned to wait until you came back out, but I wasn't sure you had any more to hang out."

"But you are overseas."

Luke moved up to the washer and started handing clothes out of the cold rinse water to her so she could run them through the ringer of the machine. "That was rescheduled. They need pilots trained to fly the new helicopters. Our group went to Texas for training. We'll be leaving for Europe in two weeks. I wanted to see you before I ship out."

"Oh," came her weak reply.

He frowned. "You've lost weight."

Rayanne didn't know how to respond. What had Amber told him?

When she didn't answer he let the garment he was holding drop into the water and took her hand. "I've thought about you a lot and have been worried that…" He paused and took a breath. "The truth is there could have been consequences from our night together. I don't have a lot of time and I need to make sure you're okay before I leave."

"What do you mean?" Rayanne stammered.

"Let's finish this wash and go someplace where we can talk. You don't want someone, especially your landlady, seeing me here."

He was right. Rayanne had enough on her plate as it was. She didn't need an immediate eviction. She quickly finished the load and emptied the washer. Deciding to leave the way she was and without her purse, she followed Luke through the backyard.

****

Luke held the door to the Buick as Rayanne slid in. She had lost a lot of weight. He would guess at least fifteen pounds, and she had a slight built to start with. He turned the key in the ignition and decided to use the weight loss to start the conversation he guessed she didn't want. "So, you've lost weight and you don't look well."

"Wow! Just what a woman wants to hear. It's

August. The hot weather is always hard for me."

Luke glanced over at her. His gaze held hers for a few beats. Maybe he'd better wait until they got someplace so he wasn't driving because they were going to have this conversation. He'd spent too many nights thinking about her, wondering how she was, who she was with. How could she have become so important after only one date? Luke didn't understand it, but he was drawn to her. And, now seeing the dark circles under her eyes, he was more worried. She wasn't well; that was for sure.

Changing the subject, he asked, "Been doing any dancing?" As soon as the words left his mouth, he wanted to suck them back. With nothing safe to talk about he fell silent. She did the same and kept her eyes on the floorboards in front of her.

When he turned off the road into the park she glanced up. He shrugged. "Good as place as any to have our talk."

He saw Rayanne swallow, and if anything, she looked paler. Hoping she wouldn't get sick or pass out on him he hurried around the car to open her door. "You okay. Would you rather go someplace else?"

Again, she swallowed, and his gaze flew to her lips. Even with dark circles under her eyes and almost no color in her face, she was beautiful. Though now she had an ethereal look, like a soft wind could blow her away. He fought the urge to take her in his arms and assure her he would take care of everything. Damn testosterone. He had more than his share. But she wasn't a typical damsel in distress, and if what he was now almost certain of was true, she hadn't gotten to where she was on her own. As he watched, she visibly pulled herself together. He had to admire her courage and only hoped it, and pride, wouldn't prevent her from taking what he had to offer.

She followed him over to a picnic table. "Good enough?" he asked.

At her nod he waited for her to swing her legs over the seat, and then went around to the other side where he could watch for anyone coming up from the parking lot. "I should have stopped to get something to drink. Sorry, I never thought about it."

When her face turned almost green, he'd bet she was thinking of all the beer they'd drank the last time they were here.

"I'm okay."

"You are anything but okay. In fact, you look like you'd rather be anywhere but here. Or is it you'd rather be with anyone but me?"

Ignoring his question, she asked, "Why are you here?"

"I told you; they sent us to Texas."

"I mean *here*," she stammered.

She had purposely kept her head turned away from him. First in the car and now looking down where she was tightly clasping her hands on the table. Reaching over he took both her hands in one of his. They were cold. In August? He brought up his other hand to try and give her some of his heat. "Look at me, honey. I know you are pregnant."

He sat forward trying to hear her low, soft voice. "I'm so ashamed."

Luke closed his eyes as her words hit him like a bullet, and he imagined they were just as painful in their own way. When he opened his eyes and looked across the table, he saw one lone tear roll down her cheek and his heart hurt for her. She was so young. Twenty-one to his almost thirty: worse, she was decades younger in experience. He felt like crying himself.

Taking a deep breath, he said, "Please look at me."

Slowly she raised her gaze to his. Her eyes were shiny with unshed tears and he again marveled at her courage. It was clear that she hadn't wanted him to know she was carrying his child, and just as clear that she intended to go it alone. Well, that wasn't going to happen.

He released one of his hands and ran it down his face. "You have nothing to be ashamed about. I'm proud of you. You are a strong, brave woman trying to make life work when it is stacked against you. Someday, women won't need a man like they do now."

He paused, taking another deep breath. "A damn good thing too since we're a huge part of the problem. And, if anyone should be ashamed it's me. You're young and—"

Before he could finish, she pulled her hands away from his and put them in her lap. "I'm not that young. Twenty-one isn't young, Luca."

She surprised him using his real name. Few people did. Or, if they did, they got it wrong. It was a family name from his father's Italian heritage and one he didn't intend to hand down to his son. Pulling his mind back to the current, he said, "Age is one thing; experience is another. I should have had control and protected you."

He waited for her to say something and kicked himself for not picking up some soda. It was getting warm out and his mouth felt dry. Making a decision, he got up from the table. "Come on. Let's run back downtown and find a place to get a drink."

Rayanne looked like she wanted to object, but then seemed to think better of it.

A few minutes later Luke pulled in front of a root beer drive-in. "Do you want curbside or would you rather go in?"

"Let's sit out here."

He placed orders for two root beer floats. Turning in his seat he looked over at Rayanne. She still wouldn't look at him, and he needed to start talking, or better yet, get her to talk to him. Did she have plans? Would her parents help her? He knew that whether or not she would take his help really depended on what her options were. Drawing in a deep breath he went for broke. "I saw Amber yesterday and she said you worked last night so I know you need to get some sleep. While you do that, I'll run back up to the base and talk to the chaplain about when we can get married."

He'd talked in a low voice but it sounded like he had shouted the words. Finally, he had finally gotten Rayanne's attention. Her head whipped around, and she stared at him.

"What? You have a better plan?"

When she didn't answer he shook his head. "Okay, from the look on your face, I take it you don't want to marry me. Will your parents help you?"

For a minute he didn't think she was going to answer him, then in almost a whisper she said, "My mother passed away."

Damn. "How long ago?"

"Eight months."

"That's when you started working for the telephone company?"

Their root beer floats came and Luke took one from the tray the girl had attached to his window and handed it over to Rayanne.

Her voice was still low and he had to lean in close to hear her. She thanked him and then said, "I started working for them a couple of weeks after mom died, and moved in with Amber when I got my first paycheck."

"What about your father?"

Rayanne shook her head. Like before a closed look fell over her face. Damn, she would never make a poker player. A good thing, because it didn't take much to read her.

"Have you thought about what you're going to do in the months ahead. I mean it's obvious you don't want to marry me. Were you at least going to let me know? I mean you must have thought I would help with support."

"I don't even know you, Luca."

"Well, there is that. But it's still hard to think you feel that I wouldn't want to know."

****

Rayanne took another sip of her float. She couldn't remember the last time she'd had one, and it tasted so good. When Luke had said what he had about marriage she'd felt a lift of the something heavy that had settled over her since she'd finally fully accepted that she was pregnant. It had only lasted maybe a second before reality crashed in. If—and for just a minute she had let herself think about the "if"—they got married she didn't have to go further than her parents to know how much he would come to resent her, and worse the baby. Keeping her head down she pushed words out of her mouth. "I didn't see any reason to tell you. I thought you were already overseas fighting this war. How would your knowing help me?"

Luke looked like he wanted to erupt. "Okay. Then you weren't planning on me helping. What *were* you planning?"

He looked like he was holding his breath, waiting for her answer. She didn't have to wonder what he was thinking. "I'm not going to abort the baby."

A smile touched his lips making him look younger. "I didn't want to think that."

"Are you catholic?"

"No, but I was raised going to church, just haven't been getting there much lately."

It was evident in the way he was looking at her that he was waiting for her to say more. With a sigh she resigned herself. He wasn't going away until they settled this between them.

"Thank you for offering, but I'll be okay. I'm pretty sure I can get through another three months. That will mean I'll be five months along. I plan to quit before they notice. Even if it's four months, I will have enough saved."

"Have you been to the doctor?"

Why did it seem so natural for him to ask these personal questions, and more to the point, why did she feel okay answering him? "No. But I will."

"Sooner rather than later. You no doubt need vitamins."

Rayanne made the mistake of glancing over at him and immediately made eye contact. Not good. She felt her pulse speed up and immediately ducked her head down. "I know I don't look healthy, but it's just this morning sickness. And that should be about over."

"Morning sickness?" He looked skeptical.

Rayanne couldn't help the little laugh that escaped. "Okay, so it's more like all day sickness. Lucky me, huh?"

They finished their floats and the girl came out to pick up the empties and take the tray off the car window. As soon as she was away from the car, Luke reached over and put his hand over Rayanne's where they lay clenched in her lap. He gave them a soft squeeze before starting the car. "Where to?"

"I don't work tonight, but I'm getting tired. Could you take me home, please?"

The day was warming up and the car had gotten hot sitting at the root beer place. Rayanne didn't do well in heat at the best of times, and this wasn't one of them. Luke had just gotten on the road when she gasped for him to pull over. The car barely stopped when she opened the door and almost fell out. Bending over she lost all of the root beer float until all that was left was bile. And still, she couldn't stop heaving. Luke was at her side almost immediately and this time she was thankful for the support. Without it she was sure she would have been laying in the ditch.

He helped her back to the car and squatted down beside her open door. "Good grief, no wonder you don't look well."

"It isn't always this bad. I'm sorry you had to see this."

Rayanne rested her head against the back of the seat and closed her eyes. Luke didn't make any move to close the door. Instead, he stayed where he was. "You can't do this by yourself, honey. Nor should you. Let me help."

Rayanne didn't want to move, she was so tired. And right at this minute she felt calm and at peace. If only she could just go to sleep and wake up to the end of this nightmare. Luke was a good man, one any woman would want to marry, but she knew only too well the path a forced marriage followed. Just before dying her mother had shown Rayanne a picture. In it were a good-looking man and woman in their late teens. She had told Rayanne the picture had been taken before they had gotten married, that her father hadn't always been the man Rayanne knew. Her mother had struggled, but finally told Rayanne that she had gotten pregnant and neither had been ready for marriage. Her father had plans to join the Navy and travel. All of sudden he was stuck in a nowhere job.

Rayanne knew she couldn't live the life her mother had, always reminded of how she'd trapped Luke into a mundane life he'd never wanted. And what about the baby. She deserved better.

Chapter 3

Rayanne felt better by the time Luke pulled up in front of her apartment building. He hadn't said anything on the way, but he didn't look happy. She had the door open before Luke could turn off the car. There was nothing more to say as far as she was concerned. All she wanted was to get up to the apartment before she collapsed.

Luke seemed to have a different idea and hurried around the car. "Wait, we can't leave this like we're doing."

Rayanne took a couple of steps toward the house and then turned back. "Luke, we have to. I have to. Thank you for checking in on me. Most guys wouldn't have." Again, she started toward the house.

Luke stepped in front of her. "Okay, I obviously can't force you to marry me. But at least tell me what you plan to do." He took a breath and whispered, "Please."

This wasn't fair. Luke meant well and he was willing, well more like insistent, to take responsibility. With a sigh she turned back toward the car. She had to sit down before she fell down. Luke rushed around to open her door and then, like before, squatted down in front of her.

She closed her eyes for a minute. She had to make this short and try to give him closure. "Like I said, I'm planning to work for another three months and save as much as I can."

"What about after the baby comes?"

This part he wasn't going to like. She could almost see him figuring on coming back and being a part of his baby's life even if she wouldn't let him be a part of hers. She glanced down at her hands. No way could she look at him. "You're right. I can never earn enough to take care of a baby. Plus, when the war is over and men start returning, it will be harder for women to find work."

Luke nodded.

"There are homes for…" She took a breath and hazarded a glance over at Luke. His gaze found hers and she could almost hear time ticking. Finally, she broke eye contact and started again. "There are homes for women like me. Especially if I agree to give the baby up for adoption."

Again, she glanced over at Luke. This time he had his eyes closed. "You want to give the baby away?" he choked out.

"Nothing about this is what I want, Luke."

"Then don't. Marry me. Think, Rayanne. I'm not going to be around for maybe a long time. Married to a man in the military, you and the baby will have good, even great medical benefits. You'll get a housing allowance. You won't even need to worry about being a wife. Well except if you want to write to me." His voice dropped. "And I'd surely like that."

He stopped, letting his words sink in. When she kept her head down, he whispered, "More importantly, the baby will have a name." He didn't have to say what the child would be called without marriage. She knew.

"Thank you, but I just can't."

"Are you worried about when I come home? I might not you know, and if that happens the baby will continue to get support."

She tensed, and before she could say anything, Luke stood up and held out his hand to help her out of the car. "You've about had it. Think about what I've said. And Rayanne, think hard, because even though we don't know each other I'd bet once you hold this baby you are not going to be able to give it away."

He took her by surprise when he bent down and kissed her on the cheek. "I'll see you tomorrow at noon. Try to get some sleep."

Rayanne put her hand over her cheek where it felt warm from the brief contact with his lips. He really was a good man. If only. As she made her way inside the house, she thought back to what Luke had said about how she wouldn't be able to give the baby up. Would it have Luke's dark hair and beautiful eyes? Squaring her shoulders, she willed back tears.

****

Rayanne buttered her toast, hoping it would stay down. The apartment was quiet with Amber at work. It had been two days since Luke had left her at the front door. She hadn't met him the next day like he'd planned. He'd tried calling, but she hadn't taken the calls. Still, she'd done nothing else but think about Luke and his proposal. If she married him her life would be so much easier. And, Luke himself? Her heart beat faster just thinking about him. But she'd seen firsthand how these situations just did not work out. No. It was better this way. Better to cut things off than live with a lifetime of resentment and even hatred.

For now, she needed to avoid seeing or talking to him. It was proving harder because Amber was seeing Noah again. To further complicate things she didn't support Rayanne's plan. Instead, she spent every minute she got the chance to, trying to talk Rayanne into reconsidering.

Just before Amber left for work, she'd told Rayanne that she was making a huge mistake and that if she thought Noah was half the man Luke was, she'd work on getting pregnant herself. "And, you can bet I'd say 'yes' to a proposal."

Rayanne glanced at the clock and realized she needed to hurry if she was going to get to work on time. Thankfully it was within walking distance. One of the main reasons keeping this apartment was important.

Not wasting time, Rayanne walked at a fast pace. Even faster than usual. Going to work at eleven o'clock at night was scary, and tonight she felt an ominous premonition. By the time she got to the telephone company she was sticky with sweat. Worse, she didn't feel good. Why couldn't she just have morning sickness like other women? Why did it have to last twenty-four hours?

She had just entered the building when she saw Amber and another woman walking toward her and realized that with their shift over, hers had started. She opened her mouth to say hi and all of sudden it felt like the hall was receding. It was dark like the power had gone out. She reached for the wall to steady herself and then nothing—

Rayanne could hear Amber's voice, but it sounded like she was down a tunnel. She tried to open her eyes. She was so sick.

31

"Help, me. We have to get her up before someone sees her." Amber's voice was low but held a note of panic.

Another voice, Rayanne remembered there was another woman with Amber. She forced herself to open her eyes and a very worried looking Amber came into focus.

"You had me scared. Can you stand up?"

The other woman, Rayanne couldn't for the life of her remember her name, said, "She can't go into the switchboard room. Berniece will know immediately and even if she doesn't want to, she'll have to report this."

"I know. Let me think for a minute."

"She doesn't have a minute. Take her home and when you get there call in and say she is running a temperature and that you're sure she has caught this flu that is going around."

Amber put her arm around Rayanne's waist and walked her back down the hall to the door. Once out in the cool air Rayanne felt herself reviving. "I'm okay now. I can go to work."

"Believe me, you don't want to do that. You don't have a bit of color in your face, and if you pass out again you are going to wake up without a job."

The other woman nodded. "You were lucky we got out a little before the others."

As if on cue the rest of the shift filed down the hall. Laughing and kidding back and forth the three women weren't seen at first. Then the swing shift supervisor spotted them. "You're late," she said, addressing Rayanne."

Before Rayanne could say anything, Amber did.

"We were trying to talk her into going back home. She looks like she's running a fever."

The supervisor moved closer. "You don't look flushed. In fact, just the opposite." Her eyes widened as if a light bulb came on, and she whirled away, mumbling. "No doubt it is the flu. We don't want anyone else getting it."

"Right." Before anyone else could get a good look at Rayanne, Amber took her arm and quickly walked her away from the group. Once they were a good block away, Amber slowed down. "That was close. Let's get home and call you in for sick."

"Do you think your supervisor will report this?" Rayanne's voice was shaky.

"I don't know."

By the time they walked back to the apartment, Rayanne felt better. "I hate missing work. I'm going to need all the money I can save and this won't help."

"Do you think you had a choice? Go call so you can forget about going in."

Rayanne nodded and made fast work of calling. When she came back in Amber was waiting for her. "You know you're going to have to go to the doctor. And soon. I can't believe being this sick is part of having a baby."

Up to this time they hadn't spoken the words and now they hit Rayanne like a freight train. Just saying "having a baby" made it real. All too real. "What am I going to do?" She sank down on the sofa.

Amber went into the kitchen and came back with a cold glass of water. "Here. You know what you need to do. Luke is right and you're darn lucky to have a guy like him."

"But we don't know each other. He will come to hate me when he comes home and feels trapped."

"Maybe he won't."

Rayanne laid her head back on the sofa. He would. She knew he would.

Amber sat down beside her. "Right now, you need to take care of things and leave worrying about what if's for later. For one thing, with all of the hasty marriages I wouldn't be surprised to see a lot of divorces when this war is over. It wouldn't be the stigma it is now."

Silence filled the room as Amber's words filled Rayanne's thoughts. She was right, and if through all of this she could at least find friendship with Luke they might have an amenable separation. One where they could both be good parents and still move on with their lives. Oh, she was so confused.

"Well, you can't do anything more tonight. Or I should say morning it's almost one o'clock."

Amber was right. What kind of friend was she? Sitting up Rayanne said, "Go on to bed. I'll take the couch."

When Amber hesitated, Rayanne got up from the sofa and took her arm moving her toward the bedroom. "Go on, remember this is my daytime."

With that Amber laughed and started across the room toward the bed, but stopped when both women heard the phone ringing out in the hall.

"Uh oh." Amber beat Rayanne to the door and caught the phone on the third ring. They both knew there would be hell to pay if their landlady heard the phone. Or heaven forbid the other residents complained, though they both felt that the other women would like them, overlook it.

Amber handed the phone to Rayanne. Mrs. Booth, her supervisor spoke softly. "How are you feeling?"

"Better. In fact, I can come in if you need me."

"Do you think that would be a good thing?"

Rayanne didn't know what to say. Mrs. Booth didn't wait for an answer. "Let me try to make this as easy as possible for you, Rayanne."

She knows.

Nausea again welled up in Rayanne's throat. She fought it as best as she could and finally slid down the wall to sit on the floor. It was cooler, and she took a deep breath waiting for Mrs. Booth to continue.

"We are shorthanded so all three of us shift supervisors will look the other way for at least awhile. But if what happened tonight happens in front of a manager or maybe someone that would turn it in, you will be fired."

Rayanne could hear Mrs. Booth take a deep breath. "If that happens you won't be able to come back to work as your record will be flagged. If on the other hand, you resign, and I'd advise doing so because your family needs you, then if you want to re-apply for a job your record will be clean." Mrs. Booth again took a loud breath. "Do you understand?"

"Yes. I'm sorry. I really need to keep this job."

"You know that isn't possible, right?"

"Yes," Rayanne whispered.

Mrs. Booth was a kind woman. She treated all of the women on her shift fairly. Rayanne was thankful that the woman had taken the time to call her and knew if it were up to Mrs. Booth, she would cover for her as long as possible.

"Life is unfair, especially to women. Think about what I've said but don't risk your future. Mother nature, life, can be cruel and like I said you don't want what happened tonight to repeat itself in a less safe place."

Rayanne thanked her supervisor and hung up the phone. She didn't think she could move, but she couldn't stay sitting on the floor in the hall either. She pulled her knees up and rested her head on them. If only the floor would open up and swallow her, if only, if, if, if.

She felt Amber reach down and take her arm. "Come on let's get you to bed."

Amber went ahead and like earlier ran a glass of cold water for Rayanne. "Here, you still don't have any color in your face. Did she fire you?"

"No. Well sort of." She told Amber what Mrs. Booth had said.

"She really is a good egg. She's right in that you are taking a horrible risk. If you do like you say and give the baby up, you won't be able to work for the telephone company again. When the war ends and our guys start coming home there won't be as many jobs available either."

"Being on my record won't matter. I just won't use them as a reference. And, passing out hopefully won't happen again. I'm not showing so I can at least slide through for another month."

"You are taking a huge risk. Plus, you might not be showing externally but believe me you are showing." Before Rayanne could respond, Amber continued, "But, let's say you can get through one more month, then what?"

"I'll do like she said and quit with the excuse that I

am needed at home." Rayanne gave Amber a hug to soften her next words. "And don't tell Noah. You know he'll go right to Luke."

"I still think you're making a mistake. For both you and the baby. This isn't the time for a woman to be on her own. Someday maybe. Things are already starting to change."

"I'd be happy if we could just earn a decent wage," Rayanne said.

****

Rayanne wasn't kidding herself. It wasn't the lumpy sofa that was keeping her awake. She rolled over on her side. She had slept on this sofa plenty of times and it was pretty comfortable for her slight frame. No, it wasn't the sofa. She just couldn't shut her mind down. One more time she replayed what Amber had said just before they went to bed. Was she making a mistake for both the baby and herself? She didn't want to think about Luke in the equation. She didn't want him to feel cornered. Surely, he was better off getting on with his life?

Rayanne heard Amber moving around. What time was it? With her mind so full of thoughts she really hadn't imagined she would fall asleep but she obviously had.

"What time is it?" Rayanne asked as Amber walked through to the kitchen.

"Almost eleven. I'm meeting Noah at noon and we're going to hang out until time for work."

"Did you put in for a few vacation days so you could have time with him?" Rayanne asked.

"I did. I was going to tell you but then..."

"Yeah, things happened. So, when do you start

your vacation time?"

"Tomorrow is my night off and then I'll take five more off. This way I'll have six days off."

Rayanne got up and folded her blankets. Both women kept a neat house, it was one of the things that made sharing the tiny apartment work well.

"Want me to put some bread in the toaster for you?"

Rayanne wasn't ready to take the chance. "Not yet, I'll have something later. Are you and Noah planning anything?"

Amber gave an exaggerated sigh. "If our witch of a landlady didn't have so many rules, we'd hang out here but that isn't going to happen. Noah was really sweet and said he'd rather rent a room for a few days anyway, so that's what we are going to do." Amber hesitated, and then said, "Will you be all right on your own?"

"Of course I will. Besides, I'm going to take your advice."

At this Amber came back into the living room. Sounding cautious she asked, "My advice?"

"About not working anymore overtime. It was really hot out yesterday and still muggy walking in to work. You know that isn't usual for Olympia, or Washington really, as it almost always cools down at night. I'm sure that the heat, plus not getting enough sleep, brought on the event last night."

Amber plunked down on the sofa. "You are fooling yourself. I didn't say it last night, but if Irene, our landlady, gets a hint of your condition you'll have another thing to worry about."

Rayanne wanted to cry and turned to hide her face from Amber. But not fast enough. Amber got up and put her arms around her. "I hate it that I sound so mean. I wish I knew what to do to help."

A muffled chuckle sounded from Rayanne. "You try. Honestly you do, but let's face it I've made a real mess of my life." Again, she gave a half-hearted laugh. "It wasn't even hard, and took hardly any time at all to royally make a mess as big as this one."

"Oh, Rayanne, why won't you let Luke help? It isn't as if you will be living with someone you don't love. Save some money from the military support and give it to him to restart his life when he comes home. I'll bet a lot of men come home to nothing."

Amber gave her a little squeeze and apologetically said that she had to get ready. "I'll check in later to make sure you're okay."

"No, just go have some fun." As an afterthought she added, "And don't take any chances. We don't need both of us in the same boat."

"Somehow, I doubt Noah would take any responsibility. If I thought he would—" Amber slapped a hand across her forehead. "What am I saying or even thinking." Laughing she headed for the bedroom.

Rayanne puttered around the apartment after Amber left. Finally needing to do something productive she mixed up a pan of brownies. When what should have been a delicious scent made her stomach roll, she decided to try and catch a little more sleep. No matter what, she couldn't afford a repeat of the night before.

A knock on the door woke her up. Hoping it wasn't the landlady, she opened the door to her neighbor. "There's a call for you," she said as she handed Rayanne a piece of paper. Frowning, she added, "We knew this would be coming."

Miss Irene, as the landlady wanted to be called, didn't like them using the telephone. She had one in her apartment and allowed for a common one in the second-floor hall. The tenants were all aware of it being conveniently placed so that all she had to do was step out her door to hear at least one side of the conversation. They also suspected that she listened in on the party line.

Rayanne hurried over to the phone. She would read the notice later, though she could guess that it was a reminder to limit phone usage.

It was Amber and her voice was barely above a whisper. "Thankfully I don't hear another receiver being picked up but I'm going to monitor what I say just to be safe."

"What do you mean?"

"You know how we talked about what could happen here at work?" Amber paused. "Well, everything we talked about this morning is happening."

Rayanne felt bile rise in her throat and choked it down. Thankfully she hadn't eaten anything.

Amber paused and then said, "Meet me at the side door. I get a break at eight o'clock."

Rayanne started to say something but Amber interrupted. "Just do it."

The phone went dead and all Rayanne could manage was to stare at it. Thankfully the other tenant had gone back to her room to give Rayanne privacy. Feeling sick, Rayanne went back to her apartment. It was only five o'clock. Amber had barely gotten to work.

Time crawled by until it was seven and Rayanne could leave. This time she was giving herself plenty of time to walk slowly. Unlike the night before the evening was cool with a refreshing breeze. She was about two blocks away from the telephone company when a car pulled up to the curb. Thinking it was probably just a guy or guys flirting Rayanne quickened her steps. When the car kept even with her, she glanced over. The passenger's window was down and Luke leaned over so she could see him better.

"Get in."

"I've only got a little way to go." Rayanne kept walking.

"Damn it, Rayanne. You have to be the most stubborn woman ever born. Get in the car."

When she didn't answer, he pulled up ahead of her and was out the door in a second. "You want to make a scene?" His jaw clenched.

When he opened the passenger door Rayanne didn't see much of an alternative. The last thing she needed was to, as he said, make a scene. Especially this close to work.

When Luke got back behind the wheel, he took a breath and reached to put the car in gear.

Rayanne glanced over at him. "So, was all this just a ruse? Amber doesn't want to talk to me?"

Luke left the car in park and rested his forehead on the steering wheel. Rayanne could barely hear his words. "I wish. Noah called and told me what's happening. Rayanne, you have to listen. Amber loves you, and I care about you."

Rayanne stopped him from saying anything further. "What do you mean, what's happening?"

With a sigh Luke started the car. "Talk to Amber, then we'll talk." He looked over at her and said, "And, this time you're going to listen."

The side door of the telephone company opened, and Amber stepped out. Rayanne opened her door and hurried across the parking lot.

Amber motioned for Rayanne to join her in the shadow of the building. "I don't want to be seen. And, it's important that you're not."

"What do you mean?"

"Last night got out somehow. This place is nothing but a gossip mill."

Somehow Rayanne wasn't surprised, or at least she knew she shouldn't be. Something like this had happened just after she started work at the phone company. Of course, she hadn't known the girl, but from what Rayanne heard she was nice to everyone. If women couldn't even stick together…

Amber looked like she wanted to cry. "I hate this, Rayanne. Mrs. Booth was here when I came to work." She dug in her pocket and pulled out a piece of paper. Handing it to Rayanne, she said, "She is going to help you."

"Help me. How? I don't want her to get in trouble."

"Look, you are going to have to stop doing this all on your own and let people help you. This is what she said." Amber held up her fingers and ticked one of them. "First, call her at the number on the paper. She said to find a phone where you won't be overheard. She will say that you called to let her know that you have to quit your job due to being needed at home. The phone company knows your mother passed away just a few months ago. This way your employment record will be clean—"

"Someone had to have seen me pass out."

"Mrs. Booth said if asked, and she's sure she will be, she'll tell them you've been trying to take care of family stuff while working overtime and it got to be too much. She also said that will further explain why you are quitting without notice."

What a mess. Rayanne felt numb but had the presence of mind to thank Amber and tell her to get back inside so she'd have time to eat at least a little of her lunch. Walking back across what seemed a mile of parking lot she couldn't get her mind to work. Luke had been watching and walked around to open her door.

Silence filled the car. Luke knew more than he should, and it didn't take much to know how he'd found out. Amber had never been for Rayanne not accepting his help. She wondered what Noah thought about it all. Probably glad it wasn't him in the mess Luke was in. Well, it was his own fault. She'd tried to keep him out of it. Now she didn't have a choice.

Rayanne's voice was barely above a whisper. After a few words, she looked straight at Luke and tried again. His gaze caught with hers and held. For a second, she felt lost. Then she said, "Okay. I give up. But I know you are going to wish you'd left well enough alone when you had the chance."

Chapter 4

Luke didn't like the way Rayanne looked. It was like she wasn't really there; like she was in a world of her own. He didn't like any of it, but especially didn't like not knowing what to do. "You're not going to be sick?" he asked.

"No. I'm okay and I should have been expecting that this would all come out." Looking around she sat up straighter. "Where are we going?"

"Someplace where we can talk. I'd take you home but—"

Rayanne took the opportunity to change the subject to their living problems. "I know, Amber has been talking about getting another place. Somewhere she can have friends in."

And, no doubt men, Luke thought. He didn't have any delusions about Amber and Noah. They were both out to enjoy life in the party way. It just had never been something he enjoyed a lot of. Oh, he liked going out with a pretty girl as much as the next guy, but not every night or even every weekend. If he had a choice, he much preferred a good movie and maybe a nice dinner with a few drinks. And, of course, he loved flying and working around planes.

"I need to use a telephone, but not at the apartment," Rayanne said.

"Another place of gossip?"

"No, the other tenants are really nice but Miss Irene, our landlady, is nosy. *Really* nosy. It wouldn't do to have her hear even my half of the conversation." Rayanne hesitated and then brought him up to date on the night before and told him what Amber had said.

Luke pulled his mind back to the issue of the minute. "Sounds like you at least caught a break with your supervisor."

"I did. And with you. I know I haven't made it easy for you. Most men would have walked away, giving thanks they were off the hook."

Luke reached over and took her hand. "I'm the reason for your troubles."

"That's not how people think about it. You know what they call women like me?"

Anger surged through Luke. "Well, I'd better not hear them."

A few minutes later Luke pulled into a motel parking lot. "Help me look for number fifteen. Noah rented it for a few days. Thinking we were going straight overseas he sold his car. It's no trouble catching a ride to and from base, but once in town there's no place to go except a bar."

Or the woods, he thought, remembering that night. "A good thing right now, because he gave me the key so we could use it."

"Use it?" Rayanne's voice gave away what she was thinking.

"To talk. And for you to make that phone call." Luke forced himself to relax. One of them needed to lighten up, and with all that must be going on in Rayanne's mind he needed to step up to the plate.

Relief that Amber and Noah weren't there filled

Luke as he opened the door and snapped on the light. The room was small but clean. He motioned for Rayanne to have a seat at the table. "Might as well get that call in. Would you like me to step outside to give you some privacy?"

Rayanne shrugged. "No need now. I suspect you know everything there is to know. Amber has made no secret of the fact that she disagrees with the way I'm managing this."

There wasn't much Luke could say. She was right in that. Noah had been keeping him in the loop through Amber. He nodded and sat down on the bed. "You do realize that we all care about you, right?"

"I wish…" She looked like she was fighting tears. And, why not? Physically sick, not enough money saved to see her through, now no job. She must feel like she was backed into a corner. Luke wished he had more time, but time was running out. After he left, she would be on her own. It would be bad under any circumstance but being sick to the point of passing out made it a hundred times worse.

Luke's voice was soft with sympathy, and he'd just bet she was taking it as pity. "Go ahead and get the call over with. Then we'll talk."

****

Rayanne slowly hung up the phone. Mrs. Booth had told her the plan pretty much as Amber had said. She wouldn't need to go back into work, so more lies on her part. Mrs. Booth had told her they would give her final check to Amber and Rayanne confirmed that was okay. With another door closed to her, Rayanne felt empty and strangely detached.

Luke brought her back to the present when he

scooted closer and took her hand. "Good. One thing off your list."

"Not good, but you're right. Maybe I need to make a list. It might help me assess where I am."

Luke smiled. She wasn't so detached that she didn't notice how it transformed his face from handsome to—something else. She wanted—she wasn't sure what she wanted. For a second her heart seemed to stop. Could he maybe care about her? No, she had to get control of her attraction to him. He was an honorable man and what he felt was responsibility.

Luke stood up and took his wallet out, extracting a piece of paper. "Not to worry. Because I've made one."

The room was suddenly warm. Rayanne hoped it wasn't a prelude to getting sick again. "Does it feel warm in here to you?"

"It is a little warm. Do you want me to open a window?"

"No, I'm okay." She didn't want to be a bother.

Luke shook his head. "Have you always been this stubborn?" He walked around the bed and opened the window a crack and then walked into the bathroom coming back with a glass of water, which he handed to Rayanne.

She watched as Luke sat down in the second chair and pulled it closer to the table. He looked at his list. "I talked to the chaplain."

Rayanne briefly closed her eyes as shame washed over her. She wished this would go away, that she would wake up and it had all been a nightmare. Almost immediately guilt filled her. Was she wishing the baby away? Until just a few days ago she hadn't given much thought to the little life nestled inside her.

Luke hesitated for just a second then continued. "We have to get this sorted out. It isn't like you're taking anything from me—"

She interrupted, *"Not taking anything from you.* What do you mean? Luke, unless you haven't been listening, I don't have any money and no way of supporting myself. In fact, I have, let's see, one hundred and thirty-three dollars in my bank account."

"I've been listening." He didn't say it, but she still heard the words. *You are the one that hasn't been listening.* "What I mean is, I get a housing allowance that I wouldn't get when I am single, so it isn't taking anything out of my pocket."

"I'm sorry," Rayanne managed to get out.

"It's okay. I understand that you feel rushed and maybe like the control is being taken from you. If I had more time…" He held up his hand displaying his fingers. "We were told to plan on fifteen days to get our affairs in order. After that we will be confined to base in prep for departure. This is the third day and it's over, so we have twelve days left. There is a three-day waiting period after we apply for a marriage license." Luke paused.

She knew he was giving her time to respond, but she didn't know what to say. Finally words she hadn't planned echoed in the room. "What's in all this for you?"

Luke shot up so fast his chair banged against the wall. Gritting his teeth, he ground out, "You know, I've tried to be patient, to give you time to come around to all of this. But I'm hitting a brick wall at every turn. From the start you haven't wanted anything to do with me. I know that night wasn't a dream, but you aren't all innocent either. And you know what? I'm done beating my head against a wall." He pulled open the door and stood back.

"Where are we going?" Rayanne couldn't believe the shaky sound of her voice.

"Where do you want to go?" Luke growled.

Rayanne didn't answer and instead lifted her head and marched out of the door, right past Luke's car and out to the road.

"What do you think you're doing?" Luke said in a loud whisper.

"I can walk from here." Rayanne kept her voice down as well. It was after midnight and the last thing they needed was for someone to call the police.

She heard Luke's sigh of relief as she looked up and saw Noah and Amber coming across the parking lot. Amber stopped by Rayanne, and throwing up his hands, Luke told Noah how glad he was to see them.

"Trouble in paradise?" Noah asked, in a loud enough voice for Rayanne and Amber to hear.

"You might say that. Or more like trouble in hell. I should have taken your advice and stayed out of this."

"Yeah. You shoulda. But come on Luke, you aren't that guy."

"Well, it doesn't look like I have much of a choice."

Rayanne felt the tears burn down her face and tried to stop crying. Finally, with a hiccup, she let Amber put her arms around her. "What am I going to do?" she sobbed.

Amber gave Rayanne a squeeze and stepped back far enough to see her. "Did you find one of those homes you talked about?"

"Not yet. And I'm not sure they will take me this early. That wasn't a problem when I was going to work for at least two more months but now…"

"I'm sure Luke will send you money to help."

Rayanne sobbed harder. "I don't think so now. For one thing it wouldn't be fair. He explained how he would get a housing allowance if we were married. If not, it would have to come out of his income. And I can't do that to him."

"You may have to."

The men were still standing just outside the door. It really wasn't much of a walk back to her apartment. Rayanne walked further in the dark when she went to work. "I'm going to go home. We can't stand out here."

"Are you sure?" Amber asked.

With a weary sigh, Rayanne said, "I'm not sure of anything right now."

****

Rayanne woke up to a crick in her neck, and no wonder as she'd fallen asleep sitting on the sofa. The last time she'd looked at the clock it had been five in the morning. She should have gone into the bed at that point. With Amber out, the apartment was all hers. Feeling achy she got up, stretched, and headed for the bathroom. One look in the mirror and she wished she hadn't. Her eyes were red and puffy from all the crying the night before. After she'd gotten inside the apartment, she'd let it all out. They say you feel better after a good cry, but she could attest to that not being true. It felt like she was adrift in a very big ocean.

She needed coffee and a shower. And in that order. But she was hesitant about the coffee. She rarely kept it down these days. Finally deciding to give it a try

Rayanne made for the kitchen. As the coffee perked, she thought about the plans she had formulated while lying awake. Now, if only Luke would give them one more try. And, that was one very big if. At least she had a plan A and B. And, he *had* followed her home last night to make sure she was safe. So that had to be a good sign.

She poured a cup and was just taking it back to the bathroom when she heard the phone in the hall ring. Hurrying out, she breathed a, "Hello."

"Rayanne?"

She recognized Luke's voice and felt a moment of excitement mingled with relief. "Yes? Thank you for calling. I wasn't sure I'd hear from you again."

"And, I'm betting you wouldn't have called me."

"I don't know," she stammered.

"I'll be out in front of your apartment in an hour. If you've changed your mind about marrying me, be out there. If you're not, I'll take it as a 'no.'"

"Okay. I'd like to talk to you first though. I did a lot of thinking last night."

****

Rayanne hurried through her shower and felt better even though she knew she didn't look like it. Not even makeup could help. Though if Amber were here, Rayanne would borrow some from her and have her help apply it. Rayanne took one last look in the mirror and headed for the door.

It wasn't early, but she was extra quiet. The last person she wanted to run into was Miss Irene. When she heard the downstairs apartment door squeak open, she bit back a curse. Wasn't she ever going to catch a break? At least she was early. Luke had said an hour and she still had a good fifteen minutes.

"You didn't work last night?" Miss Irene stood with her arms crossed over her ample belly.

"No," Rayanne stated what was rather obvious.

"Lots of goings on upstairs. You know how I feel about using the telephone," Miss Irene groused.

It was apparent that her landlady was going to enjoy evicting her. Well, Rayanne wasn't surprised, and it was part of the equation in her plans.

She nodded and hurried to the door. Just as she got down the steps, Luke pulled up to the curb and put the car into park. He was such a gentleman, but before he could get out to help her in the car, she opened the door and slid into the seat.

"In a hurry this morning." Luke didn't look a lot better than she did, but at least his eyes weren't puffy— but then why would they be? She doubted he would shed any tears.

She told him about the encounter with Miss Irene, complete with a description of the gruff landlady. When Luke laughed, she felt herself relax. He had a great sense of humor. One of the things she liked about him.

This time she initiated the conversation instead of Luke. Rayanne at least owed him that. "Let's go back to the park."

"Still not ready to give in?"

"I am, but first I want to tell you that I'm sorry. You've been so very supportive and responsible. I really hate doing this to you."

"Okay, let's get things clear. You aren't doing anything to me. You didn't get pregnant by yourself. I should have protected you. As it is, I doubt I will ever drink as much as I did that night again. Guess one good thing came of it?" He laughed.

"And, as you no doubt guessed I am a very light drinker." Plus, inexperienced, she thought.

He pulled into a little café. "Let's get some breakfast. We can talk here. If nothing else, I really need coffee. I don't know what was I thinking this morning by taking off before getting at least one cup down. I need something to get me fully awake."

Rayanne was hungry, but hesitant. What if she couldn't keep it down? As if sensing her concern Luke said, "It's okay if you get sick. We'll deal with it."

He used "we" a lot. Luke really wasn't taking control of her, just the issue they were facing. And Rayanne would bet he would step back as soon as she stepped up. Well, they would see. She again thought of the plans she had made in the wee hours of the morning.

Once seated, Rayanne used caution, ordering a bowl of oatmeal with toast. At the first bite she sighed. It had been a good choice, with real cream, something that was hard to come by, and brown sugar. It tasted so good.

Luke smiled his approval.

"You were right. This is good." Again, she vowed to fully participate in talking this time. She owed it to Luke. Besides, they needed to get off on a better foot. "You mentioned your mother?"

"Yes, she has a home in Percy. After my dad got out of the military, he went to work for the railroad, so she has his pension. Not a lot, but she has always been a good manager so is pretty comfortable."

They made "getting to know you" small talk, with Rayanne asking questions. He told her about growing up an only child. It sounded like a perfect family. Nothing like hers. If he agreed to her terms, her baby would be a part of this family. At the thought, longing surged through her. She didn't know how it felt to be unconditionally loved.

She had almost finished her breakfast and decided she'd had enough. For the first time in weeks her stomach felt full and settled at the same time. Rare these days. Luke had ordered her tea instead of coffee and she took a sip.

Now or never.

"I couldn't sleep last night so instead I made a couple of plans." Rayanne took a small tablet out of her purse.

"A couple huh? Does that mean you're going to give me a choice?" Luke smiled, taking any bite out of his words.

"You will always have a choice." Rayanne was serious and try as she might she couldn't muster up more than a weak smile.

Luke pushed his plate away. He looked a little wary as he waited for her to say more. Not wanting to give Rayanne a chance to withdraw again, he motioned for the waitress to take their plates and refill his coffee. When they were again by themselves, he said, "Go on, I'm listening."

Rayanne played with the handle on her cup keeping her eyes down. "I know you aren't ready to settle down with a family. You love what you do and maybe you didn't ever want to have children, but for me, I have always wanted someone and now with mom gone I feel so alone."

She drew in a breath, but before she could continue

Luke spoke up. "Why wouldn't you think I'd want a family? Maybe not now, but someday. Being an only child can be lonely for a guy too."

"I guess I just thought… anyway, my first choice would be to keep the baby. If you could help financially, I will keep track of the amount and pay you back. Sort of like an unofficial loan."

The look on Luke's face gave away the anger he was trying to contain. Before he could say anything, she said, "I don't mean it like it sounds."

"How do you mean it?"

His question gave her pause. How did she mean it? From his point of view, she could understand his anger.

She tried to smile, but knew it fell short. "You're right. I'm grateful that you want to support the baby, but I'm going to need more than child support for a while." She made a note on the notebook in front of her. "If you agree to the overall plan we can decide on the details. Like say fifty dollars a month for child support. Anything over that, I'll do like I said and keep track of it so that I can pay it back."

When Luke just sat there staring at her she knew he had processed what she said and didn't like it. Finally, keeping his voice low, he asked, "Do you plan on giving me visitation rights?"

Relief flooded through Rayanne. "Oh, of course. Like I said, we can iron out all the details."

"Umm, like getting a divorce without ever marrying?"

"Something like that," Rayanne stammered.

"I don't like plan A. What was plan B?"

It took a bit before Rayanne could shift gears. It had looked like Luke was going to agree and all of her thoughts was on how to manage the relationship.

When she didn't answer him, Luke said, "You didn't have a plan B, did you?"

Rayanne looked down, fiddling with her cup of tea, while Luke waited somewhat patiently. Finally, she mumbled out, "With no job and soon no place to live I guess plan B is to get married."

"Gee, swell, you make me feel so loved. Do you really hate the idea of marrying me? Is it me, or marriage itself?"

Hurt had replaced Luke's anger and Rayanne felt a twinge in the region of her heart. Of all the guys, she'd had the luck to find a really good man. "You are one man in a million. You don't deserve any of this."

"And you do?"

"Maybe not, I'm hoping someday I will think back and know that this child, who I already love is the best thing that has ever happened to me."

Luke reached over the table and took her hand. "Me too," he whispered.

Reaching over he picked up the bill. "Let's get out of here. One way or another, we've got some work to do today."

Chapter 5

Luke again pulled the car into a space in the park. It was beginning to feel like home. Rayanne hadn't said anything on the way and the silence had given him time to think things through. Her plan A wasn't really so far off from getting married. Maybe not a traditional love and forever marriage, but one of convenience, more like a business arrangement.

"Do you want to maybe walk down to the water?" Luke asked.

Rayanne readily agreed. Probably to escape the closeness in the car. She wasn't good for his ego that was for sure. Until her, he'd never had any trouble drawing girls, and then women's, attention.

They walked in silence. Strangely, it wasn't uncomfortable. Luke liked Rayanne. He ticked off what he liked in his mind. She was honest, had good work ethics, was a good friend—which meant loyal to his way of thinking. She certainly took responsibility. To sum it up she had integrity and he felt like he could trust her. He drew in a breath as his body, if not his mind, took in what else he liked. She was beautiful. He might have had too much to drink that night, but he remembered how she felt in his arms. His body hardened with just the thought. He remembered her scent, clean, and not a cloying perfume like so many women wore.

His steps slowed as relief surged when he saw a bench on a grassy section just above the beach. He pointed to it, and Rayanne walked ahead of him toward the spot. From his vantage point he couldn't help but notice how the slacks she was wearing hugged her shapely form. He almost groaned.

Luke had noticed the effort Rayanne took this morning to not only participate in the conversation, but to initiate it. A part of him wished she were more experienced, but he quickly altered that sentiment. Trusting her was priceless in this situation. He'd just bet his mother would love her. Pulling his mind back to where they were right now, he sat down, giving her plenty of room. "To get back to our—what do we call it? Issue, situation?" He laughed.

"Well, it is both of those for sure. So, what do you think of plan A?" she asked.

It looked like she was holding her breath as she waited for his answer. A cool breeze came from the bay in front of them. It was a beautiful morning, promising another warm day. Relaxing to try to put her at ease, he turned toward her. Putting his arm along the back of the bench, he said, "I think it's a good plan."

"You do?"

"You sound surprised."

"No. Yes. I guess I am?"

Luke laughed, a real one this time. "You are beyond priceless. I don't know if I've ever met anyone as honest as you are."

"Thank you. I feel the same way about you."

This time Luke didn't have to work to relax. They might very well have more in common than either of them thought. "Friends?"

"Oh yes, thank you." Her voice faltered.

Luke fought to not take her in his arms. What he was feeling was a great deal more than friendship. Pulling himself together, he said, "What you are proposing is like a business marriage without the legalities of an actual marriage."

Rayanne nodded. "You describe it better than I did."

"Let's say we agree to this plan." Luke paused as he saw Rayanne's response. She would never make a poker player. Hope, and more, spread across her face and body. For the first time he felt good, like the man he'd been raised to be.

Making himself draw back from the acute emotions swirling around them, he continued. "Did you bring your paper and pencil?"

Rayanne nodded as she pulled both out of her pocket. With their heads together they discussed and wrote down the amount of child support and the amount she would need to live on until the baby was old enough for her to go back to work.

"There are so many unknowns, like the amount for rent and utilities and medical," Rayanne said as she looked at the list.

"Yes, but we can probably make a pretty good guess on say the rent."

An hour later they sat back both satisfied with a tentative budget. Luke took a deep breath and decided to plunge into *his* plan for them. "You're plan A is good but—" He stopped, how could he word this and keep their fragile communication going?

Rayanne made it easy when she smiled and said, "Go ahead. I'm not surprised that there is a 'but.'"

"First, do you trust me?" he asked.

"Yes," came the simple reply.

He let out the breath he hadn't realized he had been holding. Then he repeated what he had said earlier. "What you proposed is to have a business marriage without the legalities of an actual marriage. Right?"

At her nod he continued, "If we revise that plan with a legal marriage that is platonic, we would have the benefit of military support. You and the baby would have access to the base commissary, medical, a housing allowance, even schooling if you want to go back and get more education."

When she didn't say anything, he continued. Lowering his voice, he said, "I'm not trying to insert drama here, but we have to be realistic. I may not come home."

At the look on her face, he held up his hand. "Hey, I plan to. But it's pretty nasty over there and if that happens, you want the baby to—"

Rayanne's eyes filled with tears and she held up her hand to stop him. "Please, I hear what you're saying."

"Then?" he asked.

"You're right. I promise to do my part in this. I'll save as much as I can so that when you come home, you'll have something to start on. But…"

Luke laughed, "Ah yes, the 'but.'"

Rayanne didn't join him in seeing the humor and he waited as she worked at forming words.

"I need one promise," she whispered.

Luke nodded.

"First, I want to tell you something so that you'll understand how very important this is to me."

Again. Luke only managed a nod.

"I didn't grow up in a home like you did. My parents hated each other, *really* hated each other. I can't remember a time they didn't. But there must have been a time." Rayanne looked up and met Luke's intense gaze. "I'm betting you are wondering how I got here if that was always the case with them."

"You don't have to do this." Luke shifted uncomfortably.

"I do, but it will take longer than you and I have to give you a full picture of how we lived. I was in high school when mom got sick. Really sick. She had always been obsessed with her health. Each of my parents had their own way to cope with their lifestyle. Anyway, this time it was for real. Cancer. They gave her maybe a year and she lived two. Just before she died, she showed me a picture. I didn't recognize the two nice-looking people. Mom told me it was her and dad. I couldn't believe it. Then she told me that it was her fault that he hated her. He was planning to join the navy and get a college degree. She couldn't let that happen so she told him she was pregnant."

Rayanne's voice dropped so that Luke had to bend forward to catch her next words. "She told me it was a lie. That she hadn't been pregnant. She had trapped him into an instant marriage." Rayanne paused, her continued in almost a whisper. "By that time though she was almost three months along with me. And of course, dad was no fool. He could add. He never forgave her."

Rayanne looked down to where her hands were tightly clasped in her lap. "He never escaped. Mom never worked and always played weak and sick so that he wouldn't leave her."

Luke reached over and took her hands in his. "You are not your parents. That's all behind you. Hopefully your father will find happiness. But it has nothing to do with us. I won't feel trapped with you."

"You don't know that. And that's why I need your promise that when you come home, we *will* get a divorce."

"What about the baby?"

"I will do everything I can to be independent so it won't affect your plans for the future by placing a financial burden on you. Your place in his or her life will be up to you."

Luke bit back words he wanted to say, deciding to let the future take care of itself. "Swell. So, we're okay until I come home for good?"

Rayanne swallowed as if she might be sick. Then said, "One more thing. If you find someone and want to be free, you have to let me know."

"What about you?"

"I'll be okay."

"Boy you really know how to boost a guy's ego. I meant, what about if you fall for someone?"

Rayanne shook her head. "That isn't going to happen. For one thing, very shortly I'm going to be fat and pregnant. There are a lot of women out there, and no guy will want someone in my condition."

Luke couldn't believe it. How did Rayanne not know how beautiful she was? She looked like a picture with her dark mahogany hair that emphasized green eyes with long lashes. There would be guys. He'd bet on it. Deciding not to point all this out to her, he instead said, "Still I want your promise too."

When she gave it, Luke wasn't sure if he was

relieved or worried.

****

Luke took Rayanne's arm as they left the courthouse. Three days until the wedding. He was pretty sure she wouldn't change her mind, but he wasn't positive. He'd feel better if there weren't a waiting period. At least she was looking better this morning. He could only imagine the weight that was off her shoulders. He hoped all they had to do before he left wouldn't put it right back on.

He glanced at his watch. Almost noon. "Are you hungry? Want to catch a bite to eat?"

"I could use something to drink, but I'll bet you're hungry. What time did you eat breakfast?"

"I was in a hurry so skipped it." Luke motioned to a soda fountain sign across the street.

Seated, Luke waited for Rayanne to scan the menu. He had already decided on a hamburger, a staple for him.

"Could I just have a strawberry milkshake?" she asked.

"You can have anything you want. I'll even share my fries with you."

"Deal."

Luke relaxed. He enjoyed being with Rayanne. Maybe too much. "Have you thought about where you want to live?" He hated breaking the mood, but there was so darn much to do before he left for overseas.

"Amber and I have been talking about finding another place, but it isn't easy to find something we can afford."

"What about moving away from Olympia? I grew up in Percy. My mother still lives there and really likes it. It's closer to the base so you would have easy access to medical and the commissary. They also have a telephone company so maybe Amber could get on there."

"If we could get a place close enough to walk that might work, but I doubt Amber will want to give up the social life she has here."

Luke nodded. Amber, and for that matter Noah, liked the single party life. "Umm, you're probably right. Let me check around and see if I can find anything for you."

Rayanne sipped the milkshake. Again, Luke noticed how much better she looked. No doubt a good night's sleep helped.

"You are doing enough. I have a little saved up."

Luke swallowed a bite of his burger and wiped his mouth. "I don't want to push you and I wouldn't if there was more time, but as it is, I'll feel better if you're settled into something before I leave."

When she didn't say anything, he was a little surprised. Encouraged, he continued. "Please, I know if our places were reversed, you'd feel the same."

No sooner than the words left his mouth and Rayanne started laughing. When she caught her breath she managed, an "I'm sorry. Oh my, heaven help us if you were in my position." She burst out laughing again.

Luke didn't think it was that funny, but was enjoying every second of her humor. He finished his hamburger and pushed the fries toward Rayanne. "Here, finish these. I'm going to get a cup of coffee."

"Do you get a headache when you don't have caffeine?"

Luke liked how they were doing this morning.

And, he liked her. A lot. "I do. And, thinking of 'I do,' we need to talk about the actual ceremony. Do you have an idea of what you would like?"

"I would feel... I don't know, maybe feel dishonest if we had a religious wedding? Or even if we invited anyone." Rayanne looked over at Luke then added, "What about your mother? You said you went to church with her..." Her voice tapered off and she looked down at her hands.

"We don't have to share everything. To the world, outside of maybe Amber and Noah, no one knows about the baby. In this case we can use the limited time I have before shipping out as the reason for a civil ceremony."

The relief that fell over Rayanne's face gave Luke more hope and he continued, "What do you say about returning to the courthouse and making an appointment with the judge for Friday, if today counts as one of the three waiting days. If not, then on Saturday?"

"Okay." She didn't sound sure, but at least she didn't bolt. "I'm thinking Amber will go with us to be a witness. Do you think Noah would?"

"Swell idea. We'll run by their motel room after we make the appointment with the judge. They should be up by then."

****

Rayanne was exhausted and it was still early in the day. Why couldn't she be one of those women who went through pregnancy easily? Being sick was the worst, but being tired all the time was a close second. Plus, she couldn't help but think that a lot of people thought she was lazy. She didn't want Luke to think that of her and was determined to put on a cheerful persona with hopefully more energy than she felt.

Amber and Noah had just gotten back from breakfast or lunch when they arrived. Both seemed delighted to witness their wedding. With that out of the way Luke looked happy and an almost festive mood filled the room. Amber was bursting with fun and had everyone laughing at the stories she told of the night before at one her favorite late-night places. She snuggled up to Noah and with a teasing flip of her hair said, "Why don't we have a double wedding."

Silence fell over the room until Noah put a joking spin on what she had just said. "No time, love. Maybe next time I'm home."

He might have been joking but Rayanne could tell Amber wasn't. Rayanne would have traded places with Amber in a heartbeat. As soon as the thought entered her mind, she knew she wouldn't want that. As much as Rayanne loved her friend, she was sure Amber didn't have the staying power when it came to commitment and men. From the short time they had roomed together Rayanne had seen Amber with a number of different guys, seemingly enjoying them all. It was amazing in light of how different they were that they were such good friends. Age might have had something to do with it. Amber was closer to Luke's age. Rayanne guessed that Noah was also about the same age. All three of them, well except maybe Luke, treated her like a little sister.

Luke broke into her thoughts. "Ready to get moving?"

Had he noticed that she was tiring? She hoped not.

Ever the gentleman Luke opened her car door. Starting the car, he said, "I need to get back to base and start the paperwork to declare you as a dependent, so we can start getting housing allowance. And get your ID papers so you can get on base for medical and the commissary."

He looked over at her and grinned. "You are going to love the commissary. We'll make time to go shopping there before I go."

Rayanne wasn't sure if it was fatigue or the fast pace of the day, but she was glad Luke was taking care of things for them. The idea of a nap sounded like heaven.

When they pulled up in front of her building Miss Irene, the landlady, was coming down the steps with her usual scowl. Luke put his hand over Rayanne's where they lay in her lap. "Pretend she isn't there. Before I go, I'll do everything I can to find you another place to live."

"Really, Luke, you have done so much. Don't waste anymore of this precious time with me. Instead spend it with your mother and friends." She started to open her door but then turned back to Luke. "I'll see you Saturday morning."

His hand on her arm stopped her. "Not so fast. We need to get rings plus a few other things."

"I don't need a ring."

"I do and I want you to have one." A stubborn looked replaced his smile.

With a sigh Rayanne nodded.

"So, I'll pick you up tomorrow at noon. Try and sleep in for once."

Sleep in for once. Luke made her feel cared for. And, maybe even loved. At the thought Rayanne tamped down the hope swelling around her heart. She needed to be strong. If she started having hopes it would be harder to let him go when the time came.

The next day was clear and Rayanne felt like a new person. She hoped she would never have to work a graveyard shift again. Then felt immediately guilty. With Luke supporting her she should be happy to get any shift so she wouldn't be a burden on him. Rested, she took her time getting breakfast which consisted of toast and honey. An hour later, still in her nightgown, she marveled that her breakfast had stayed down. Could all this morning, or all-day sickness have been in part because of stress?

She was out on the front steps when Luke pulled up to the curb. Smiling he got out of the car and walked toward her. Her breath caught. He looked like a hero in the movies—in fact, *better*. When he reached her, he was careful to keep a respectful distance. "Ready? I thought we'd pick out rings and then take a drive to get an idea of housing."

"Oh, Luke, like I said yesterday, you've done so much."

Before she could say more, he put his finger over her lips. "Let me be the judge of that. You'll be on your own soon enough, and I'll be flying, which I love."

Rayanne didn't know about that. News from overseas didn't sound good. Luke wasn't going into a fun adventure. He was going to war. The closer it got to the time for him to leave, the stronger her fear for his safety became. Deciding that for the rest of their time she would do it his way, she said as much and got a beautiful smile in return.

Thinking Luke would drive to downtown Olympia she was surprised when he headed out of town. Reading her thoughts, he said, "I grew up in Percy and know the family that owns the jewelry store there. Is that okay with you?"

"Sure, I haven't ever been to Percy."

"What about when you were in high school? It's only about twenty-five miles and our schools competed, especially in baseball."

Rayanne shook her head. "By the time I was in high school mother was sick, so I didn't have your usual school experiences."

"No boyfriends?" Luke joked.

"And, no time," she quipped back.

It didn't take long to get to Percy and Rayanne enjoyed every minute of the ride. Luke made "getting to know you" small talk. She found out that there was only his mother and him. Like her, he had no siblings. He did have cousins and an aunt, his mother's sister.

"Do your cousins and aunt live close to your mother?"

"Yes, they live in Tacoma. I'll take you over an introduce you before I go if we have time."

Rayanne's heart thudded. She didn't want to get too close with his family. This wasn't a real marriage. A little voice seemed to whisper, *it's a real baby and this is his or her family.* Feeling selfish that she would deny their baby the family Luke could offer and she couldn't, she reached over and touched his hand where it rested on the gear shift. "I'd like that, if you have time."

"I'll try to make time."

Percy was a lot smaller town than Olympia with a slower community feel about it that Rayanne found appealing. Luke parked the car in front of a jewelry store. "Here we are."

Rayanne hadn't thought ahead to things like rings. Nothing felt real to her yet. Not even the baby, though it was beginning to. She forced a smile as Luke helped her out of the car. As soon as they opened the store's door an older man put down the ring he was inspecting and walked around the counter. "My gosh Luke, it's been forever. It's good to see you."

Luke introduced Rayanne saying, "I grew up with Mr. Harris's son, Gary."

A smile lit up Mr. Harris's face. "Yes, and let me tell you, they were a formidable pair on the baseball field."

While Luke and Mr. Harris caught up on things, Rayanne browsed the display cases. Her attention returned to them when Luke called her over. "I was just telling Mr. Harris that we are getting married and looking at rings."

The older man beamed at her. "Luke here tells me he is heading overseas and he doesn't want to wait until he gets back to get married. I have to say it's about time. Gary has two kids with another on the way, so Luke has some catching up to do."

Rayanne felt her face get warm and could imagine how pink it no doubt was. Luke saved her from replying to Mr. Harris by directing her toward a case with rings in it.

There was quite a selection for so small a store but then Rayanne had never really shopped for jewelry, so she really hadn't known what to expect. Looking over at the jeweler she said, "I think bands would be best."

"Ah, a good choice. Many young people prefer the bands." He took a large tray out from the case. "Look them over. I'll be right over there when you're ready."

Rayanne saw one she liked right away but was scared it would be too expensive. Luke followed her gaze and picked up the rings. "You like this one?"

Mr. Harris came around to the counter. "Good choice. It's white gold and the etchings are a unique design."

"We'll take them," Luke said.

Rayanne put her hand on his arm. "Wait." Turning to Mr. Harris, she asked the price.

"For Luke, all the rings in this case are the same."

Mr. Harris took their sizes and said the rings would be ready by noon the next day.

"And just like that the rings are taken care of." Luke laughed as he walked her to the car.

"But aren't you worried about cost?"

"Not if I'm doing business here, I'm not. And you shouldn't be either."

Rayanne stopped at the car door that Luke held open. She had to remember that this wasn't real. It was only pretend. So why did she keep feeling butterflies even when she worked so hard to hold back any excitement. Luke's gaze held hers until he dipped his head and kissed her lips. Soft like a feather but oh so sweet. "Thank you," she whispered.

Luke backed out of the parking space and started down the street. "Are you ready to meet my mother?"

Rayanne was never going to be ready, but it was high time she started giving back. Taking a breath, she told him, "Sure."

"Sure, you're not." He laughed, reaching for her hand. "Don't worry. She will love you."

Chapter 6

As they drove along a tree lined street Rayanne admired the neighborhood. The houses weren't grand, but they were well maintained. Unlike where she had grown up. She wondered what Luke would say about her father's place and fought a shudder at the reception they would no doubt get.

"This is nice."

"Mom and Dad moved here when I started school. I was ten when my dad died. A train accident."

"I'm sorry."

Luke squeezed her hand. "It was a long time ago."

"Your mother never remarried." It wasn't a question and immediately Rayanne was sorry she'd said anything more, reminding herself again that this wasn't a real marriage.

As if he could read her thoughts he glanced over and pulled to the curb. "Mom's house is on the next street. If we are going to pull this off, you are going to have to get better at pretending. Or did I miss something when we decided to present a united front for the baby?"

"I'm sorry." Rayanne looked up and met his gaze. "I'm going to do better. I know you've been carrying the whole load up to now. I'm surprised you haven't given up on me."

Luke turned off the car and silence fell around

them. "Would you rather tell at least my mother the truth?" He quickly added, "Not today but before I leave."

"No," she stammered.

"Okay, we'll try it. I'm sure she is going to love you. As for me carrying the whole load, well let's just say if we start keeping score I'm going to fall behind."

He started the car and Rayanne swore to herself that she would start acting like a grown woman, soon to be a mother. His words had hit home. He felt responsible because he was older, but only eight years. She started to say something about their age difference but before she could, they pulled into the driveway of a neat looking house with green shutters.

"This is it." Luke smiled over at her, and her heart gave a little flutter. He was so darn good looking. She felt like pinching herself to make sure this wasn't all a dream. In the course of just a few days she had gone from the depths of disaster, sick, almost broke, not knowing what she was going to do, to a safe haven. Now if only she could hang on to it all.

****

Annie Accardo straightened her skirt and opened the door. Luca had called earlier and told her he was bringing someone special to meet her. He hadn't given her much notice, but she had managed to put a much-coveted roast in the oven, and bake an apple pie. She hated the idea of Luca being deployed and worry was a constant companion for her even though she tried to cling to her faith that he would be safe. Hah, was anyone safe overseas fighting a war? With resolve she pasted a smile on her face and stepped out on the porch.

Luke and a beautiful young lady were coming up

the walk. Annie put her hand over her heart. Oh my, she hadn't expected this; He had brought some of his military buddies to visit a time or two and if she thought about it at all she would think he might bring a couple of guys with him today.

Luke put his arm around the young lady and pulled her closer. "Mom, I want you to meet Rayanne Meyer, soon to be Rayanne Accardo."

Annie swallowed a couple of times trying to find her voice. Finally, she gave up and just put her arms around the young woman, giving her a hug. It was apparent in the way the young woman stiffened that she wasn't used to hugs. Pulling back, Annie smiled trying to put the girl—*woman*, she corrected her thoughts, at ease.

"Oh my, Luca. You might have warned me. This is a surprise." At the look on the girl's face, she quickly added, "A very happy one."

As soon as Luke stepped in the door, he took a deep breath. "It smells like a piece of heaven in here."

"Pot roast and apple pie." Annie motioned for them to be seated. "And you're darn lucky with all the notice you gave me." She smiled putting her words in place.

"I know mom and I'm sorry. Things have been crazy since I got back from training. And, I have so little time before we ship out."

"I know." Annie did know and worried. Smiling over at the girl, Rayanne— she had to stop thinking of her as a girl—she lightened her tone, "Are you from around here?"

****

"I grew up on the west side of Olympia." Rayanne again resolved to act the part of a woman about to be married and continued with answering Luke's mother before she asked the next question. "Luke and I met a few months ago. Actually, our friends introduced us. Sort of a blind date."

Annie offered them coffee and tea. When she got up to get it, Luke suggested they all go to the kitchen. He turned to Rayanne. "The kitchen table has always been our gathering place."

"Was it that way at your home Rayanne?" Annie asked.

Rayanne shook her head. She couldn't ever remember sitting at the kitchen table for anything other than eating. If her father had ever joined them, she didn't have a memory of it. "It was mostly just mom and me. My father worked a lot."

To Rayanne's relief the conversation moved to the wedding. Luke took over and Rayanne relaxed. The affection between him and his mother was apparent. As long as Rayanne didn't hurt him, she felt she would have a friend in her mother-in-law.

"It's going to be a simple wedding. There just isn't time for more," Luke said as he finished with the wedding plans.

"Have you thought about waiting until you get back?" Annie asked.

Luke reached over and took Rayanne's hand. He didn't say "if he got back" but the unsaid words hung in the air. Luke didn't answer her question, instead he changed the subject. "Rayanne lives in a woman's apartment house. They aren't even allowed to invite men in for a visit so we will need to find a place to live."

"Why don't you just maybe stay in a hotel for the

few days before you leave?"

Of course, that made logical sense from Luke's mother's view.

"I'd rather see her settled before I go," Luke said.

Annie didn't argue. Instead, she said, "Mr. Pierce just finished some beginner's homes. He purposely built them for young couples starting out."

"Did he add to the development he has?"

Annie cradled her cup in her hands. "No, this is a new community, but it is only a few blocks away. Over by the school."

Luke turned to Rayanne. "Do you want to take a walk?"

Annie said that she would stay and get dinner ready so they could eat when they got back. As they walked down the street Rayanne felt better than she had in too long. She liked Luke's mother and loved the neighborhood. Luke took her hand and said, "Just in case anyone is watching."

Rayanne smiled up at him. Pretending was turning out to be fun. Soon they turned into what looked like rows of look-alike small houses. The colors were neutral but some had shutters for design and some even had window boxes which added color. The lawns were small but green. The shrubs and trees were still young but Rayanne could see where they would give a distinct look to the homes as they grew.

"What do you think?" Luke asked.

"I like them. They are so clean and neat. It looks like a happy place."

"It doesn't take much to make you happy, does it? What do you like about this development?"

Rayanne thought on what he said. She guessed he

was right, but to her this was a lot. Again, she thought of what he would say if she took him out to her father's place.

Luke looked down and winked. "Don't let me spoil this for you. I'm happy it takes so little for you. Let's walk down to the end and see if there are any empty homes."

Rayanne like that he called the houses, homes. She wanted to imagine living here and making friends. Something she'd never been able to do growing up.

A man came out of one the houses on the end. He looked to be about the same age as Luke's mother. Luke greeted him. Did he know everyone in town? It wasn't that small though it gave off a small-town feel or what Rayanne imagined a small town would be like. The houses and street were so different from where she lived now that it could be in a different world.

"Hi Luke. I hear you are about to join the fighting in Europe." The man had a deep voice with a trace of an accent.

"I am, but first I'm getting married," Luke replied. He put his arm around Rayanne's waist and introduced them.

Mr. Pierce, or Galen as he asked her to call him, said, "Ah and maybe you're looking for a place to call home. These would be nice for your bride. Especially so close to your mother, hey?"

He pointed to two houses on a cul-de-sac. "We just finished these. They are open so go on in. If you're interested give me a call." He handed them a business card and wished them a good day.

"Wow. He is really trusting," Rayanne said.

"He's known me my whole life. He and my dad

were friends." Luke took her hand as they went up the walk.

They kept saying the houses were small, but to Rayanne it looked big compared to the apartment she shared with Amber. The front door of the first house opened into a fair-sized living room. On the right were two bedrooms with a bath in the middle. On the left there was a door to the kitchen that had room for a table.

Luke nodded toward a door on the other side of the kitchen. "Looks like a utility room for washing and this one even has an attached garage. What do you think?"

Rayanne drew in a deep breath. "I love it. But it must cost a lot."

"I don't think so, especially with a GI loan."

"GI loan?" Rayanne didn't know a thing about buying a house. She hadn't even rented one as Amber had taken care of the apartment rental.

"It's a new program introduced by Republican Harry Colmery just this year. It allows veterans to purchase a home with lower interest and mortgage payments and most of the time without a down payment. It will be a good investment for us."

Rayanne liked the sound of "for us." She looked at the house with a new view. Could she make it a home for Luke to come back to? A smile spread across her face at the thought. In order to take advantage of an investment like this, Luke would need her help. Just the idea made her feel good.

"Let's look at the other house. You might like it better."

This one was right next door. The front door opened into the living room like the other one, but the kitchen was behind it with a back-porch type of utility room for a washing machine. The two bedrooms were to the right, but the bath was on the end with a little hall that had storage cabinets. Rayanne liked both of them. They were brand new, something she'd never dreamed she would live in.

"What do you think?" Luke asked.

"I love them both. Which one do you like?"

"How about going back to mom's and we can think about it during dinner. Both have good things about them. I kind of like having a garage."

Rayanne nodded. She would be happy with which ever house Luke chose.

****

"More roast?" Luke's mother passed the platter to him.

He put it down without taking anymore. "I can't eat another bite. This was delicious." He'd noticed that Rayanne seemed to have more appetite than she'd had. Hopefully the sickness was behind her.

"Then how about some coffee?"

"Maybe a half a cup," Rayanne responded, again leaving Luke hopeful that the worst of the pregnancy sickness was behind her.

Settled, with coffee in front of them, Luke brought up the subject of the house. They had talked a little during dinner. He knew which house he wanted but he wasn't sure about how Rayanne felt. "I would like to talk with Galen about getting one of the houses. Rayanne, do you have a favorite? And Mom, you said you'd seen both of them?"

When neither woman spoke up Luke gave an exaggerated sigh. "Swell, now neither one of you has an opinion. I should be so lucky."

His mother laughed. Looking at Rayanne, she said, "He's right. And you are going to be the one making it a home. I feel very lucky that you are sharing something so big with me, but the decision should be between the two of you." She stood up and made a shooing motion. "Why don't you take your coffee out to the porch and talk this over."

Luke, very aware of his limited time, thanked her. "But let us help you clear up first."

"Nonsense. Go."

Settled on the porch swing Luke waited for Rayanne to say something. It took her a bit but finally she said, "I love them both. Should we find out if they cost the same?"

"I can do that. Either is move-in ready. The first one has wood floors all through it and I don't know how that will work in the kitchen and bath, but we could have linoleum put in." He thought for a second and then said, "I'm leaning toward the first one with the garage."

At Rayanne's radiant smile he knew he'd picked the right one. "If that one's okay for you I'll run back down and try and find Galen. He may be home for his own dinner by now."

"Is it okay if I tell your mother which house we chose?"

He smiled. "Swell, because we'll need to get going when I get back and she is going to so excited that we can't just tell her and take right off."

The ride back to Rayanne's apartment didn't seem to take as long. When she mentioned as much, Luke laughed. "It always seems that way. And, we did have a lot to talk about coming back."

Rayanne didn't reply and Luke glanced over at her. "You okay? I mean you do want to move to Percy, right?" As soon as the words left his mouth, he got a cameo view of the day and doubts throbbed through him. She hadn't actually said she wanted to move away from Olympia at all. In fact, as he looked back at the past few days, she must have felt like a steam roller had entered her life. He had to admit that the machine had his name written all over it. How in the devil had he let himself get carried away like this? And now, he had all but signed on the dotted line to purchase a house.

Silence filled the car. Luke wanted—no, more like *needed* to think this through. In his rush to make things right had he taken over her life? And, had he unknowingly done it for himself instead of for her and the baby? If he were being completely honest, he liked the idea of a family. His cousins were both married and were making a marriage and military life work. He had been giving settling down some thought. He was getting tired of the single life. Damn, had he unknowingly used Rayanne?

When they got to Rayanne's apartment, he turned off the car but didn't move to get out. "I need to talk to you," he said.

She looked wary as she waited for him to continue. She was just a kid. Couldn't he have gotten involved with someone like Amber? Yeah, and what were the chances he'd come home to her waiting for him. He knew that there would be an influx of divorces after this war was over, but in the past few days hope that his wouldn't be one of them had started taking root.

Luke shifted so he could look at Rayanne. "I've been thinking," he began and stopped. She looked like she was fighting tears.

"You're sorry, aren't you?" Rayanne whispered.

"What do you mean?"

"Oh, Luke. I tried to tell you this wouldn't work. I am getting a whole new life, and I'm ruining yours."

"Is that what you think?" Luke's voice deepened.

Night had fallen and there was an intimacy in the car that made Luke want to take Rayanne in his arms and tell her that she had brought a light into his life that he hadn't known was missing.

"Are you happy with this new life?" he asked.

"Not if you will be unhappy and—"

Luke reached over and took her hand pulling her toward him on the seat. "And what, honey? Do I look unhappy? I've got a lot on my mind, but I'm not unhappy. So, what else did you start to say?"

Rayanne lowered her gaze to their joined hands. "My mother and father hated each other. They lived in the same house but rarely talked."

"They probably talked when you weren't around, like in bed."

Rayanne shook her head. "No, they didn't. For one thing he slept on the sofa and I know he hated her."

Rayanne raised her head and met his gaze. He bit back a curse at the sadness he saw in her eyes.

"Mother said that she purposely trapped him and he never got over it. Like me, she didn't have any family and he was a man that had been raised to do the honorable thing."

Again, silence filled the air. Luke put his forehead against Rayanne's. "And, you think this is the same?

Me being honorable?"

When she didn't answer Luke took a breath. He wasn't sure he could put into words what he was feeling. Or for that matter if there were any words Rayanne would believe when he wasn't sure just how he felt himself.

He took a deep breath. In for a penny, in for a pound. "I knew, of course that you weren't comfortable with our arrangement. I thought it was that you were feeling pushed. Like control of your life was being taken away. I warned myself to slow down but I really can't. In a little over a week, you will be on your own. Anything I can do before I leave, I want to do. It's my choice, Rayanne."

Rayanne's voice was still barely above a whisper. "I'm afraid that as soon as you have time to catch your breath, you're going to resent me. Even hate me."

"I won't. For one thing you've made it very clear that I'm free and that you will help me in any way you can to go my own way at any time."

Rayanne's timid smile grew and Luke relaxed. Or at least his mind did. His body wasn't doing as well. She really was beautiful, and being happy ramped up her natural beauty until it was hard to keep his distance from her.

Luke smiled. "Swell. You'll get a breather from me tomorrow. I want to start the paperwork for the house. Galen said he's sold a number of them on the GI bill and doesn't see any problems."

He started to get out of the car when Rayanne surprised his socks off him by initiating a kiss. Experience be damned this woman could kiss. His heart rate spiked and he took over, deepening the kiss. Again, he was surprised, when her lips parted to let him in. He fought for control; thankful they were sitting in the car in full view. It wouldn't take much to fall hard for this woman. Hell, maybe he already had.

He eased away while he still could, but as a blush stole over her face, he pulled her to him again. "Thank you," he whispered.

She looked confused before blurting out, "It's me that should be saying that to you."

Before he could he comment, she had the car door open. So much for walking her to the front door. Instead, he rolled down his window and keeping any emotion out of his voice told he'd see her the day after tomorrow, but to call him if she needed anything. Then, berating himself for reading too much into the kiss, he slowly put the car in gear and drove away.

Chapter 7

Amber looked more excited than Rayanne felt. The last couple of days had flown by. She hadn't seen much of Luke, but then she hadn't expected to. The time to herself had done wonders for her own peace of mind, though. She'd made lists to help her organize her new life. And Luke had been right about feeling like control of her life was slipping away. She hadn't realized it until she'd started doing things on her own. Like packing and talking with Amber about her getting a roommate or moving down to Percy with her. She hoped Amber would, because Rayanne would miss the friendship that had grown between them. Especially over the past few months.

Rayanne had sewn a cream-colored suit for herself and never had a chance to wear it. Thankfully is still fit. With the weight she'd lost it was a little loose but nothing a few tucks here and there wouldn't take care of. Its style was the perfect wedding attire for a late morning wedding. To make it even better, Amber had found a hat at the thrift shop that looked like it had been made for the suit. Rayanne smoothed down the skirt and walked out to the living room of their small apartment catching Amber looking down at the street from the window.

"It's early yet," Rayanne said.

"How can you be so calm. Golly, if I were getting

married, I'd be jumping the Lindy Hop."

Rayanne burst out laughing at the visual. Amber looked the part with a short swingy floral dress that showed off her figure. In contrast Rayanne felt almost matronly. Should she have chosen something else? Well, too late now. The suit would have to do.

"They're here," Amber all but screamed.

They quickly left the apartment. Rayanne felt the nerves she had been holding at bay rush to the surface. Would Luke approve of what she was wearing? As they stepped out the door, Luke rounded the front of the car and doubts faded away at the look in his eyes. She'd made the right choice with the suit.

"Hey," he whispered as he took her arm. He had on his dress military uniform and she had never seen any man look better. Again, she noticed how tall and strong he was built. She had always considered her five foot four tall, but he made her feel tiny and feminine in contrast.

Noah broke in with a whistle. "You two look good enough to get married."

"You think?" Luke grinned back.

Rayanne felt like she was walking in a dream. The judge greeted them and got right to business. It wasn't a ceremony a girl dreamed about, but Rayanne was thankful it wasn't. In a matter of minutes, the judge pronounced them man and wife and congratulated them. They all signed the documents and got their copies, then slipped outside the courthouse.

Rayanne couldn't take her eyes off the ring on her finger. She loved the simplicity and intricate scroll design.

Luke broke into her musing. "I made reservations

for brunch at the Olympian." Luke looked happy himself and Rayanne hoped she'd always see that look on his face. For a second, a glimpse of her father's face over the years imposed itself in her mind, and again she vowed to never give Luke cause to hate or resent her and the baby. At the thought of the baby a feeling of love swept over her. She had made the right decision for her and the baby. And, she'd make sure it was the right one for Luke too.

When the waiter showed them to their table Rayanne was surprised to see Annie, Luke's mother. She was not so surprised to see Galen Pierce with Annie. Rayanne had felt from the beginning like there might be something more between them. Luke thanked Galen for bringing his mother. They all chose the brunch buffet and soon everyone was eating and laughing. Rayanne didn't know when she had been so happy.

"I thought about inviting your father but..." Luke's sentence hung there between them for a moment.

"Thank you, but this group is perfect. Maybe I'll try to see him after you leave. At least let him know that I'm married." *Or maybe I won't.* She really hadn't given her father any thought since she'd moved out of the house. She didn't miss him. There was nothing to miss. Well, except for the sewing machine.

The sun was out with a cooling breeze when the wedding party left the restaurant. Rayanne didn't know what the plans were from here, but guessed that Luke had it covered. She wasn't disappointed.

"You won't be able to live at the apartment much longer. I'm betting that landlady of yours already knows more than you think." Luke didn't add that he wouldn't be able to visit let alone stay, but Rayanne knew it was a given.

"Amber told me that a woman she works with is going to take my spot," she said. "They are hoping they can find something else and it's not for long. Darlene is married. He's in the army and stationed in Europe someplace. Like Amber she likes to go out."

She didn't add anything more, but was sure Luke caught the picture. Darlene and Amber were more alike but was that a good or bad thing? For now, not being able to have men at the apartment was probably a good thing.

"When will she be moving in?" Luke asked.

"As soon as possible. It will be crowded with three of us but we'll manage. Darlene works the same shift as Amber so we should be able to make it work."

Luke nodded. "Galen is okay with you moving into the house. You'll need some basics like a bed and I'm thinking at least a sofa and table set. What do you think?"

Rayanne noticed that Luke didn't say "we" even though he still had a week before he had to be on the military base. "I can get a mattress and put it on the floor for now. I have some money saved that I can use so you don't have to do more."

Luke had parked the car a couple of blocks from the restaurant. He stopped at the door. "We've gone over this before. I want to do what I can before I leave. After that it will be all on you."

"I don't want you to do more, Luke. As it is you've saved my life and—"

He put a finger over her lips silencing her. "It isn't for you. Like I said, we've already talked about this.

Maybe keep track of the money and we'll square up when I get back. It's not like I'll be somewhere I'll need money. And when I get back..." He paused, then opening the car door before continuing, "Who knows what the future holds. Let's just take care of today."

Rayanne agreed and not for the first time marveled how comfortable she felt with Luke. At first, she'd been so tense and apprehensive that she could hardly be around him, let alone engage in conversation. Of course, feeling better physically helped. She still watched what and how much she ate but except for first thing in the morning she hadn't vomited again. For a while even water had made her throw up.

"Thank you." Rayanne smiled at Luke. "I hope I don't disappoint you."

****

Disappoint him? Where had that come from? Not wanting to raise questions Luke said, "you won't," and quickly switched to the subject of moving. "I'm thinking you have a couple of choices. One, mom said you could stay with her until you are ready to move into the house. Two, I can help you get the basics and move in. We have a week to do that."

Luke watched as Rayanne thought it over. She wouldn't make a poker player that was for sure. Patience wasn't his strong suit, but he made himself wait. Finally, just as he had decided to help with the decision, she said, "Since this is your last week home, you make the decision. You must have friends to say goodbye to, and what about your aunt and cousins?"

Wow, he wasn't expecting this. An unexpected surge of emotion filled him as he absorbed that she was thinking of him, not herself. He cleared his throat. "I know this will seem strange, but I really want to help you set up the house. Mom mentioned inviting the family to come down for dinner some night before I leave but we can work around that."

"I don't know how I got so lucky to have you in my life, Luke. I know I don't show it, but I really appreciate all you're doing and I will do everything I can to earn your respect and friendship."

Her words brought Luke back to earth. He wasn't and hadn't been thinking of friendship. He reminded himself yet again that Rayanne was young and not only in age. He was too old for her in more ways than the number of birthdays. Again, he silently cautioned himself to go slow.

****

Rayanne sat down on the bed they had just finished setting up. It was either sit down or fall down. They had been going at it steady since leaving brunch. Luke had driven her back to the apartment and ignoring house rules moved her things out to the car. It hadn't been a problem to fit everything in as she didn't have much. A few days ago, she knew she would have been hesitant to let him see just how little she had, but things had changed. A lot of it just this morning. For one thing she liked Luke. Liked him a lot. She knew she should worry about how much, but he was leaving so there really wasn't any reason to give any thought to her emerging feelings. Was there?

"I'm going to get a soda. Why don't you sit here for a bit, or maybe even lay down?" Luke said softly as he left the bedroom.

It sounded like a good idea. It was almost seven o'clock and putting the bed up had been the last thing to do. At least for today. Galen had loaned them his truck and they had gone furniture shopping. Because of the limited time, they had only gotten the bed. Luke had even thought to get bedding and few things for the bathroom like soap and towels. They could stay here tonight. Rayanne's heart skipped a beat, remembering it was her wedding night. There was only the one bed and no sofa. So far Luke hadn't mentioned anything beyond the actual ceremony but—Rayanne put her hand over heart where she could feel it beating like it wanted to leave her body.

Luke was gone getting the soda for a long time and Rayanne dozed off. She startled awake when he came into the bedroom. "Ready?" he asked.

She felt out of it and tried to clear her mind. *Ready for what?*

Luke held out his hand to help her up. "Come on, you must be starved. I took the truck back and got my car. I thought we could run into town and have dinner."

Relief surfaced, and Rayanne relaxed. She hadn't even thought about food.

In the car, Luke drummed his hands on the steering wheel. Even in the short while she had known him, Rayanne was starting to read Luke's body language. He wanted to tell her something and didn't know how to begin. She smiled as she tried to think of anything she could say to make it easier on him. Finally, she said, "Maybe we should pick up something from the grocery for tomorrow morning on the way back."

"I was going to talk to you about that, and well, tonight." Luke's hands continued to tap on the steering wheel.

Rayanne glanced down at her wedding ring and

waited for him to say more. She hated that she wasn't participating, but she honestly didn't know what to say. They were married. She might be inexperienced but it didn't take experience to understand what that meant. To make matters worse she wasn't even sure she was opposed to spending the night with Luke. At least she wouldn't be if they had the option of using a sofa and bed. Like any man would agree to that? Again, the inexperience, but women talked and Rayanne was a good listener so while she may not have first-hand knowledge, she did know things.

Luke pulled up to the curb in front of a downtown restaurant. "We'll talk later."

They were seated at a table in a private alcove. Except for this morning's brunch, Rayanne hadn't been in a place as nice as this. The waiter dressed in black pants, white shirt, and black bow tie poured ice water and took their order for drinks. Luke ordered wine for both of them. "A night to celebrate." He smiled over at her.

She smiled back feeling happy, feminine, and well—loved, or at least liked. A lot. She almost felt like a bride. "We probably aren't dressed for a place like this." Rayanne glanced down at her dress.

"You look swell. Better, you're beautiful."

"Thank you," she whispered back.

The waiter came back with their wine and took their orders. Again, Luke ordered for both of them, but waited for Rayanne to approve of his choices. How had she gotten so lucky? Most men would have run for the hills, or in his case across an ocean. Especially when she had worked so hard to push him away. A premonition of the future and Luke feeling trapped invaded her thoughts, but she pushed them away this time. Not now, not ever. She wouldn't let that happen.

****

Wanting to make this first dinner special, Luke ordered an appetizer and was pleasantly surprised when Rayanne didn't object. Today, for the first time, it felt like they were a couple. It hadn't been hard for him to pretend in front of his mother and Galen. He'd caught Noah looking at him a few times but ignored his friend. He didn't know how much Rayanne had told Amber, but it didn't take much to guess Noah knew more about Luke's relationship with his wife than he would have liked.

The plate of appetizers was a variety of fried mozzarella, spinach-artichoke dip, and calamari. He knew he was probably taking a chance with the calamari but the other two selections would ensure Rayanne would enjoy the plate.

"Umm, this is so good."

Luke smiled. She hadn't had a repeat of the horrible sickness since driving the other day, or at least not while he was with her. "We probably should have quit sooner. You must be starved."

"I wasn't until now," Rayanne responded. "I'm glad we kept going. We got so much done."

"Did you get everything from the apartment?" Luke hadn't paid much attention but it didn't seem like they moved much. They had stopped at a grocery and picked up boxes. She packed while he mostly just stayed out of her way and carried the stuff down to the car. That it all fit in the car was telling.

"The apartment came furnished and Amber had it before I came along so all of the dishes, and stuff are hers."

Luke would have liked to ask her how long she'd lived with Amber but he could tell that she was uncomfortable with him knowing how little she owned. Changing the subject, he said, "I thought we could finish furnishing the house tomorrow."

Before he could say more, Rayanne spoke up. "I can make do for now."

Luke shook his head. He didn't want to mess up the mood and didn't quite know what to say. Galen had told Luke he could use Galen's truck as much as Luke needed to, and he wanted to get at least the minimum furniture like a sofa, maybe a chair, and a table set for the kitchen before he left her.

Before he could say anything, Rayanne said, "Besides tomorrow is Sunday so nothing will be open."

Damn if she wasn't right. And that he only had another week hit him. It was unbelievable what they had gotten done. Especially with the conflict in the beginning. "You're right, so what do you want to do tomorrow? We could drive out to your father's…"

Before he could finish, he knew that suggestion had been the wrong one. Rayanne put the piece of calamari she was about to try down on her plate. "Or maybe not," he finished.

Luke watched as she took a sip of her wine, then pointing to her plate she said, "What is this?"

Rayanne smiled over at him. It was apparent, that she wanted the day to continue in harmony as much as he did.

"Dip it in the marinara sauce and try it."

Trustingly, she did.

"What do you think?"

"It sort of tastes like clams."

"You're close. The word calamari comes from the Italian word for 'squid.'"

"Octopus?"

Luke laughed. "No, *squid*, but you're not alone in thinking they are the same. Actually, they are cousins." Pausing he finally risked asking, "do you like it?"

"I do." She put the rest of it her mouth and reached over the table to squeeze his hand. "This has been a special day. Thank you."

Luke captured her hand in his, liking the feel of her soft skin as he rubbed a thumb cross the top "It's been one for me too."

Rayanne's face was pink when she looked at him and quietly almost whispered, "It's not hard to pretend this is a real marriage and that we love each other."

Luke had been stopped from responding to Rayanne's surprising comment by the waiter appearing with their food. Now, after an amazing light, fun, dinner he still didn't know what he would have said.

"Thank you, Luca. I have never had a day like this one. The whole day has been swell."

Again, she used his given name and for the first time that he could remember he liked it. She asked for so little. Even on this, her wedding day. It made him wonder about her and what her life had been like growing up. She didn't talk much about herself, somehow getting him to talk instead.

Rayanne took his hand and squeezed it again. Was she sending him a message? He could feel his arousal at just the thought. Luke prided himself on his self-control. Now wasn't the time to lose it. Hell, three months ago it hadn't been the time either, and look how that turned out.

"Ready?" he asked.

When they got to the car, Luke still hadn't figured how to bring up the subject of tonight. He couldn't very well go back to the base on his wedding night. He was pretty sure they'd carried off this sham of a marriage. However, he was well aware that was not because they looked or acted so in love. No, it was more that Rayanne looked and acted like a young innocent bride. Every time someone looked at them together, Rayanne blushed. *So tonight?*

Luke was tense as he drove them back to the little house. Why hadn't he insisted on getting a sofa today. Sleeping on the floor was pretty much out of the question. There wasn't even an area rug over the hardwood floors yet.

"You're awfully quiet."

Rayanne's voice broke into his thoughts. He took her hand and looked over at her. "Just thinking."

Rayanne's laugh filled the car. "No, you're not. You are nervous."

Where had this new Rayanne come from? Whatever, she had sure picked the wrong time to get playful. It was playing havoc on his libido. "Me? Nervous?"

She bobbed her head up and down. Again, her laugh rang out. "I thought brides were supposed to have nerves?"

Was she really flirting with him?

"Now how would you know that?" he playfully volleyed back.

"I listen and women talk, you know."

Luke was getting to "like" his new wife more and

more. She was smart and could hold her own as she'd proved over dinner. He didn't know when he had enjoyed himself more. The problem wasn't in the liking, it was in the attraction that seemed to sizzle through the car. He knew he should put a stop to this kind of kidding. It was going to land them in trouble. Instead, he squeezed her hand. Then softly said, "Are you nervous?"

"Maybe a little."

Luke pulled into the driveway. Intimacy filled the car. When Rayanne slid closer on the bench seat, he all but groaned. He was in trouble.

"I might have drunk a little too much wine at dinner. It was so good," she whispered against his neck.

She hadn't had *that* much wine. For one thing he didn't think it was a good idea for her to have more than a glass. Especially since she didn't drink. "I think we should probably go back to Olympia and stay at the hotel. It's nice and a perfect place for our first night. I'm almost certain we can still get a room. Spending the day of our wedding shopping for furniture probably didn't send out the message we want." Luke's voice sounded strained even to his ears.

Rayanne nuzzled closer. "I think that fantastic dinner will send enough of a message. I'm too tired. Let's just stay here. We have everything we need except groceries, and we can get those in the morning. Besides, you have to be worn out. You did a lot of lifting."

Not tired enough, was his last thought as he took Rayanne in his arms and captured her mouth.

Chapter 8

Rayanne was immediately lost in Luca's kiss. She had made up her mind this morning that she was going to do her part. Up until then, it had all been Luke. When most men would have been congratulating themselves for a near miss, Luke was tying himself down. She wasn't going to let him, but he couldn't know that. He didn't love her. But it didn't take experience to know what he wanted. Men, unlike women, didn't seem to need "love." He wasn't heading into a good place and there was nothing she could do about that. But she could put on a loving front so that he would have at least the semblance of a traditional marriage. Except, what she was feeling wasn't a façade. It was a whole lot more than a front.

"Are you sure, Rayanne?" Luke breathed out the words.

Rayanne didn't want to talk, she just wanted Luke to continue kissing her. She closed her eyes and let passion take the reins.

"We need to slow down a bit so we can get in the house." Luke pulled away enough to look down at her.

What she saw in his eyes made her catch her breath. She had never felt beautiful and for sure never desirable. Now her body responded like it was starving.

In typical newlywed fashion Luke slid out of the car and helped Rayanne out. Then he swung her up in his arms and carried her to the house. They hadn't locked the door. Few people did in the small town. Laughing, she felt him groan in her ear when she slid down his body.

Rayanne felt alive. He might not love her but his body didn't seem to care.

Besides the bed, they had gotten some basics like bedding, towels, and kitchen things including a coffee pot. Rayanne wasn't sure where to go from here. Maybe offer him coffee? After wrestling with putting up the bed they had both showered before going out to dinner so excusing herself for that wasn't an option.

Luke caught her gaze with his. "You don't have to do this? I don't expect—"

Rayanne didn't know where this brazenness was coming from but she moved within inches of him and put two fingers over his lips shushing him. "I want to."

"You don't mean that. You're doing this because you think you owe me something." His voice dropped, "You. Don't. Owe. Me. *Anything*," he all but ground out.

Rayanne watched as frustration and anger took the place of his demeanor of just a few seconds ago. Did he not want her? Had she been wrong about assuming sex was enough for him? Before she could say anything, he turned and stormed out the door letting it bang shut behind him.

There wasn't any place to sit down in the still unfurnished house, and Rayanne desperately needed to. She leaned against the wall and slid slowly to the floor as the truth hit her. Luke didn't want any part of her. Why else would he get so angry? It was an excuse to leave her. It had to be. He couldn't have made it any clearer. She had been so sure, but then what did she know?

She wiped at the tears coursing down her cheek. If only she could be more like Amber. She was sure Amber wasn't spending the night wondering if Noah wanted her. And she wasn't even married. Not that a wedding certificate meant anything for Rayanne and Luke. It would give the baby a chance, but she needed to straighten up and figure out a plan to make it on her own because this war wasn't going to last forever and when Luke came home, she fully intended to set him free.

Rayanne got up and went into the bedroom. She didn't bother to lock the front door because no one did in this small town, right? It had nothing to do with hoping Luca would come home. It couldn't. She slipped into a nightgown, crawled into bed, and pulled the covers up tight around her neck, holding onto them like they were the only lifeline she had left. Most likely, they were.

Rayanne hadn't thought she could sleep but it had been a long day. And suddenly it was morning.

Luke had stretched an extra blanket over the bedroom window so she wasn't sure what time it was, but she could smell coffee which meant he was up. She hadn't heard him return after he'd stormed out the night before, but the other side of the bed hadn't been used. She laid there, dreading getting up and facing him. She didn't want to remember her pathetic attempt at seduction. He had sounded disgusted. Well, it wouldn't happen again she vowed as she hurriedly dressed. She would just bet there weren't many new brides that greeted their husbands fully dressed the morning after their wedding.

Rayanne was honest to a fault, but this was the time to employ some acting skills. Ones she didn't know she had until she heard herself wish Luke a cheerful good morning.

"About last night—" Luke started toward her.

Rayanne stopped before forcing a smile to take any impact from her words. "I don't want to talk about it. We were both tired."

"I do want to talk about it." Luke wasn't trying to diffuse the tension in his voice.

Rayanne walked past him and lifted the coffee pot. *What now?* Before she could say anything, a thud came from outside the front door.

"What the hell?" Luke mumbled.

Rayanne watched as Luke opened the door a scowl on his face that would scare off most people. Except his mother, who stood there with a shovel in her hand.

Annie's face was a vivid pink. "I'm so sorry. I didn't think you would be up yet."

"We are. Come on in and have coffee with us." Luke opened the door wider.

"No, I don't want to bother you," his mother stammered.

Rayanne came up beside Luke. "You're not. We were just having coffee and discussing what we were going to do with the day."

Her matter-of-fact tone must have put Luke's mother at ease because she smiled and stepped into the house. Luke poured each of them a cup of coffee and motioned to the back door. "We didn't get as much done yesterday as we would have liked. So, nowhere to sit, except for the back porch steps."

His mother nodded. "That will work. Or you could come back down to the house and I'll fix breakfast."

Luke sat down close to Rayanne. An attempt to continue the façade she was sure, but did he need to be quite so close? A fluttering low in her stomach made her shift a little. "Why the shovel?" she asked.

"I was hoping to surprise you," Luke's mother responded.

"And you don't think you did?" Luke laughed.

"Well, I sort of planned for you to see it when you left the house." Luke's mother got up and walked toward the front yard. Rayanne and Luke followed with their cups. When they got to the corner Luke drew in his breath and said, "A lilac bush." He hugged his mother and whispered, "Thank You."

Turning toward Rayanne, he continued, "My dad was in the army, and we relocated a lot. Lilacs grew most everywhere, and mom always planted one as soon as we moved in. They have a scent that we grew to associate with home."

Annie, Luke's mother, nodded as she dabbed at her eyes. "We were renting my current house when Luca died, and Luke and I stayed. A year later it came up for sale and I bought it. As you can imagine there are a number of lilac bushes in our yard."

"She doesn't want me to lose my way home," Luke teased.

Rayanne felt her eyes tear up. Another happy memory, and she would hang on especially tight to this one.

"It's been a whirlwind for you two this past week," Annie said.

"It has. This coming week isn't going to be a lot

better. I still have paperwork to get out of the way, I need to bring my civies home from the base, and we need to furnish this place a little more. I don't want to leave Rayanne with it all."

"So, you have to report back to base this Friday then?" Annie asked.

"By five o'clock."

They sat in silence for a bit before Annie whispered, "I wish this war was over. I wish…" She dabbed at her eyes. "Sorry," she mumbled.

Luke got up and pulled his mother into his arms. "Aw mom, I'll be okay. And, it won't be for long. We are getting into this thing with Germany a little late and it's almost over."

Rayanne watched from her seat on the porch. Would she have this kind of rapport with her child? Just thinking of the little life made her happy. Such a far cry from a couple of weeks ago when, knowing she couldn't keep it, she refused to think of the baby as real.

Luke and Rayanne looked at the lilac bush. It was a fair size and Rayanne was surprised that his mother had managed it until she saw the wheelbarrow. "I wanted it to bloom next spring," Annie said.

A few minutes later Annie left, telling them to take their time and she would have breakfast ready when they got down to her place.

"Wait." Luke stopped her at the drive. "What color is the lilac?"

"It's your first one, so white, of course."

Luke laughed. "Of course."

Rayanne had taken on the role of spectator. "Of course?" she asked.

"Our first one was white. Also, mom is traditional

so white for our wedding." He put his hand at her waist walking back to the door. "Let's make a list of what we still need to do. Since we can't do much more than make the list with it being Sunday, would you like to drive out to see your father and maybe introduce us?"

Just the thought dimmed the happiness of the morning for Rayanne. "Umm, no. We aren't close, Luke. I doubt he's home and I know he couldn't care less about seeing me."

Rayanne felt relief when Luke didn't pursue a visit to her dad's and instead dug out the pad and pencil he'd been carrying around. She had been surprised to see that he was a list maker, even more so than she was herself. He took their coffee cups in for refills. "Want to sit on the bed or the back porch?"

"It's so pretty outside this morning, the porch would be nice," Rayanne answered.

As they settled in to make their list, she wanted to ask him where he had slept the night before but wasn't sure she wanted to know. One more night and they would have a sofa that she could use, which would leave the bed for Luke. Rayanne could tell Luke wanted to talk about last night, and just the thought made her cringe with the memory of how she had so clumsily tried to seduce him. Before he could say anything, she started with an entry for the list.

1. Check in with Amber.

Luke frowned as he read it.

Rayanne smiled at him. "I will prioritize the list after we get it done. Knowing me and guessing about you, I'd say our list will be too long to get it all done."

"So why are we checking in with Amber?" Luke asked.

"Amber starts back to work this evening. I know she would like to take more time but she doesn't have any more vacation days."

"Umm, that will leave Noah on his own. What do you think of inviting him to stay with us?"

"Where would he sleep? Plus, we'd never fool him in believing this was a 'real' marriage." Rayanne wasn't sure she could sleep in the same bed as Luke and keep her feelings for him to herself.

"I could ask Mom if he could stay with her. She has three bedrooms and would chalk it up to us being just married with very limited time together."

Rayanne could feel her face heat up. Instead of trusting her voice, she nodded.

"So, after breakfast let's stop by the motel and hope Noah and Amber are there. I'm not sure if Noah is going to continue renting it or head back to base." Luke wrote down something on the pad.

In a few minutes they had every day filled through Friday. Luke handed the pad back over to Rayanne. "Here, all yours." His voice held a hint of humor, but it quickly faded as both of them looked at the entry for Friday and the page ending with it.

Silence settled over both of them. It wasn't uncomfortable. They didn't need to fill their time with noise. Rayanne sipped her coffee. Luke was everything she could ever want in a man, a husband, and a father for her child. As soon as these thoughts entered her head, she visualized the picture of her parents that her mother had shown her. They were about the same age as she was now and looked happy. A look she'd never seen on either of them in real life. *And that's what being trapped makes of happy.* Rayanne again vowed to do everything she could to be independent so that Luke would be free when he came home.

Luke stood up and held out his hand to Rayanne. "Breakfast awaits."

****

Luke smiled over at his mother. "Breakfast was as good as I remember. My favorite."

"It's been a while since I've made French Toast. More coffee?" His mother included Rayanne.

Luke shook his head and Rayanne said, "I'll be floating if I drink anymore. Breakfast was delicious. I've never had French Toast before. I love it. Especially with the homemade strawberry jam."

"It will be a favorite for the little one too. Luke would have eaten it every morning if I made it."

The look Rayanne gave him made Luke draw in a breath. Almost at once his mother realized what she had said. Last night, after he'd stormed out of the house, he'd gone down to his mother's. He had been trying to decide if he should tell her about the baby or not. Finally, thinking it wouldn't be long before the pregnancy was obvious and that it would be easier on Rayanne to give his mother time to get used to it, he had confided in her. Damn. At least that had been all he'd told her. As far as his mother knew they were in love and planned on forever.

Double damn, he should have told Rayanne that he'd spoken to his mother. Not that she had wanted to talk about the night before.

Rayanne recovered first. "Let me help you with the kitchen before we leave."

Thankful, Luke jumped in. "We thought we'd look up Noah and Amber." He went on to explain that

106

Amber was going back to work and they knew Noah would be at loose ends. He knew he was talking too fast as he watched the dazed look on his mother's face and the closed one on Rayanne's as she started clearing the table.

"I'd like to ask Noah to stay with us so he wouldn't have to go back to base. Would it be okay if he slept here, mom?"

"Of course." Changing the subject seemed to release his mother from the shock of what she'd said and she stopped Rayanne. "I'll get these. You two get going."

They had been driving for almost a half hour when Luke decided it was now or never. He had some explaining to do and he wanted to talk about the night before. Before he could get a word out, Rayanne interrupted him, her words cutting through his thoughts like a bayonet. "I don't want to talk about it."

"Well, this time we are going to. I—" Luke's voice was soft but firm.

Rayanne reached for her door handle. Startled, Luke slammed on the brakes. "I want out. Stop the car."

"And, what? You plan on walking back to the house?" He fought to keep from showing his anger.

"If I have to. I am not going to talk about any of this. In six days, you'll be gone and won't be able to blab about my life anymore." Rayanne shut her eyes tight as if in pain and covered her face with her hands.

Now it was impossible for Luke to hide his anger as it mixed with the hurt of hearing Rayanne's words. "Blab, is that what you think I did? You think I just blurted out that we are going to have a baby." It wasn't a question and he didn't pause long enough to give her time to answer. "You're three and half months along. How long do you think you'll be able to hide it? You think it would have been easier for you if Mom just happened to notice? And, what about her?" He took a breath and then continued, "I have news for you. Knowing my mother, she would notice that you are pregnant sooner rather than later. I'm actually surprised she didn't already know."

Silence. So now she was going to give him the silent treatment. Well, he wasn't going to let her. "What? Now you don't have anything to say?"

"I just told you. I. Don't. Want. To. Talk. About. It. Not now and not later." She glared over at him.

Rayanne turned, looking out her side window. Okay, maybe this conversation was better left alone. He wasn't sorry, for one thing, so they weren't going to agree even if he could manage an apology. He had given speaking with his mother a lot of thought, and he still felt it was his responsibility to make it as easy as possible for both of the women.

Taking a deep breath Luke took up the other subject he wanted to talk about. The wedding night. "Okay, I guess there isn't all that much more to say."

Rayanne didn't act like she'd even heard him as she kept her head turned toward the side window. Luke sighed. It appeared his wife was back to making life difficult. All anger went out of his voice as he said, "I know you think I am trying to control your life. Maybe you think I'm one of those control freaks. I'm not. In a few days you will be on your own. I know you'll have an ally in Mom if you want one, but that will be all up to you."

Rayanne finally turned back toward him. Her eyes

gleamed with unshed tears. "I'm sorry I said what I did," she stammered. "I realize this is hard for you too." She paused then said, "I'm not used to having my life become front page news. I'm a pretty private person as a rule, so it hit me hard when she knew. But... I think having your mother know will work out better. Like you said, it isn't as if I can keep something like this a secret for much longer."

Luke reached for her hand. He was surprised when she let him hold it. "And, I'm sorry I didn't talk to you before I told Mom. How about we make a pact that we will be honest with each other. I would really like to at least be friends."

Rayanne's face turned pink as she nodded. Was she thinking of their wedding night? He still wanted to talk about it. After he'd had time to think about things, he was pretty sure she thought he'd been turned off by her when just the opposite was true. This attraction was driving him nuts, but no way did he want an obligatory relationship. She didn't owe him anything, and if she had been trying to pay him for marrying and providing for her it didn't sit well with him. If that was all he wanted he could get it in town. There were always women out for a good time. Like the military men, they didn't want more than a night here and there.

Determined to push forward, Luke said, "I think we should talk about last night. We have so much between us. Having an honest, open relationship will help us move forward."

Luke was a little surprised when Rayanne spoke up. He had been prepared for more silence.

"I know that being an only child is something we have in common but from what I can see you've had a network of friends and you even have cousins. It isn't like that for me. My mother and father rarely even talked to each other. I learned to keep things to myself and pretty much lost myself in books." She took a breath and then continued, "I guess what I'm trying to say is I'm pretty much a loner. I'm sorry about last night. All I can say is it won't happen again."

Luke wanted it to happen again, and again, but he'd need to ease into that. Damn. He wished he had more than six days left. With time he was convinced he could erase any forced emotion and bring Rayanne's passionate nature to the forefront.

"You don't have to be. Alone that is. And, I'm betting you'll want the baby to have an active social life. Again, Rayanne, it is all going to be on your shoulders. Especially if you won't let my mother help you."

If Rayanne noticed he had avoided saying "a normal social life," she didn't say anything. They were on delicate footing so he needed to watch his words. She was finally talking now, and he wanted to keep this getting to know each other thing going.

"I'm going to work on it. You've given me an opportunity and I can't tell you how much I appreciate it. I really do," Rayanne said.

"You know you don't owe me anything, right?"

She shook her head. "You said to be honest and I disagree. I do owe you."

"Rayanne, you didn't get pregnant by yourself."

She held up her hand. "No, it takes two, but there is no way I will let one mistake make a life sentence for you."

"Is that how you see this? As a mistake?" His voice

was just above a whisper.

"It's different for me," she answered. "At first, I did think about how bad I had messed up. But now…"

"Now what?" Luke wanted to hear more.

"Now I want this baby. More than anything."

Luke felt his heart melt. "So do I."

It was time to turn a corner and start over. She needed some space and so did he. He took a breath and tried to find the words, but before he could she did it for him. "Let's start over. From this very minute."

Simple. He smiled over at her. "Okay."

The car again filled with silence but this time it was peaceful, almost loving, with hope for their future.

Chapter 9

Luke pulled into the motel's parking lot. There was no guarantee that Noah and Amber were even still staying there. They had been so busy these past few days that Rayanne hadn't had much of chance to talk to Amber. It would be nice if Amber could get a job at the phone company in Percy and move in with her, but Rayanne knew Amber liked to be in Olympia and she seemed happy that a co-worker was going to room with her.

The door of the motel opened almost as soon as they got out of the car. Amber hugged Luke then walked around the car to Rayanne. "You are a sight and just who we need." Amber looked back toward Luke.

He laughed. "Really. Me, or the car?"

Noah came out the door. "Smart guy. Let's walk over to the café and we'll fill you both in."

"Good gosh, you guys just getting up?" Luke asked.

Noah wiggled his eyebrows. "Something like that. We need coffee."

A few minutes later they were seated in a booth. Rayanne and Luke declined the menu but Noah said he and Amber needed substance for what they had ahead of them.

Amber playfully whopped him on the shoulder. "I don't have that much."

Noah rolled his eyes. "So she says. I have been regretting selling my car since the first minute."

"Are you moving out of the apartment? What about Darlene? I thought she was moving in with you," Rayanne asked.

"She was but when this came up, I couldn't pass on it. I am so ready to get away from that apartment and the landlady from hell." Barely drawing a breath, she continued, "Do you know who Betty Blair is?"

Rayanne nodded. "Everyone knows Betty. She is quite a character."

"That's her." Amber laughed. "Anyway, Betty just lost her roommate and offered me a room. She has a two bedroom with no house rules. We can have guests. Even spending the night. It's a little further to work but she has been walking it okay. Anyway, I can use the extra exercise." Rayanne knew she was referring to her weight which had been increasing the last few months.

"What about Darlene?" Rayanne asked again.

Amber took a drink of her coffee. "I hated to tell her, but I think she might have been relieved. In fact, she had been talking about moving back in with her parents. She said she could save money that way and maybe her husband and her could buy a house when he came home."

Luke broke in. "You're in luck. With today being Sunday it's pretty much a free day so we will be glad to help you move. Right?" he asked Rayanne.

"Sure. I'll bet our landlady is not going to be happy."

"Too bad. I've wanted out of there and so have you."

As soon as Noah took the last bite of his breakfast,

Amber was ready to get started.

"You don't have a lot of time before you have to go to work," Rayanne commented.

"No, I'm okay there. I asked for another two days off. I don't have the time coming but the swing supervisor is a jewel and said I could make it up."

Three hours later Rayanne set the mop against the wall, having mopped herself out the door. The guys and Amber had taken the loaded car over to unload and she'd stayed behind to clean. Not that she thought the landlady would give them back their cleaning deposit. She'd find some reason to keep it. Amber had wanted to leave the apartment dirty but Rayanne just couldn't do it.

Setting the mop and bucket beside the washing machine she walked around the house and sat on the front stoop. Living in the apartment hadn't been a great experience, but leaving it was like closing a chapter. In another week she would be all by herself. She'd never lived on her own before. Luke was seven years older than she was. No wonder he thought of her like a little sister that needed his protection. In large part she had herself to blame for being so inexperienced. The other single women, and some of the married ones, had asked her to go out numerous times but she'd always felt so inhibited and tongue-tied around them. She thought of the little house waiting for her and smiled. She would make it into a home, a real home for her and the baby. Luke wouldn't have to worry about them.

The car pulled up at the curb and Luke got out by himself. "You ready to go home?"

Home. A special kind of warmth filled Rayanne at Luke's use of the word. Hope, too, something that she'd tried not to give into lately.

Deciding it wasn't the right time to mention how good that one word sounded to her. She instead asked, "Where are Noah and Amber?"

"I left Noah and Amber to settle in. We have another busy day tomorrow." He paused then asked, "Is that okay with you?"

"Swell. We both could use an early night. If you stop at the grocery, I'll make us some dinner."

"Nothing will be open. Let's stop for something at a café instead."

Rayanne nodded. He was right, but this eating out every day had to be costing a lot. She thought of the piddling amount she'd managed to save and wondered, not for the first time, how she had ever thought she could manage on her own. No matter what he said, she did owe Luke.

****

As soon as they got home Luke again hung a blanket over the bedroom window for privacy. It was too early to turn in. And the attraction for Rayanne he was fighting made it almost impossible to stay close to her. The night lent an intimacy that he shouldn't test. Instead, like the night before, he took off for a walk, but this time he went in the opposite direction from his mother's house. Walking through the streets of the development he could see that even with building supplies at a premium Galen was doing well. When the war was over there would be a run-on housing, and he would be ready.

Galen fell into stride beside Luke. "Nice night for a walk."

If he wondered about Luke leaving his new wife on

a night that reflected romance, he didn't say anything. Not even to comment on the full moon. Luke opened the conversation. "You've done a great job with this development."

"Thanks."

They walked along in comfortable silence. Luke had known Galen for years. In fact, he'd worked for Galen when he was in high school, but he didn't know the man well. Galen had always seemed busy and gave the impression he was a loner. Luke could respect that.

Galen slowed his steps. Luke could tell that there was something on his mind, and finally taking a breath, Galen said, "I want to talk to you about something."

"Sure." Luke stopped and turned toward the older man.

"Man, this is hard." Galen finally managed to get out.

Luke, thinking Galen had changed his mind about the house, tried to prepare himself. Then Galen all but blurted out, "I want your permission to ask your mother to marry me."

Luke was glad he'd stopped. He wasn't sure Galen's words wouldn't have had him stumbling. "My permission?"

"I know. A little out of the norm but if you object, she'll never agree."

Luke wanted to laugh but the serious, almost pained, look on the other man's face stopped him short. "Well, you've got it. I think it's swell. In fact, what took you so long?"

Galen's laugh boomed out. "That's a good question. I guess I have always been afraid she'd turn me down and I'd lose her all together."

"So now?" Luke asked. He couldn't help but be happy for Galen and his mother. He couldn't imagine her not saying "yes." Now that he thought about it, Galen had always been around. Coffee in the morning. A glass of wine at night.

Galen answered Luke's question. "Why now? You getting married, I guess. Annie is a mother first. Maybe if you'd had brothers or sisters she wouldn't have felt so protective. Anyway, now seems right."

Luke shook his hand. "Good luck. You and Mom deserve to be happy."

Galen was whistling as he turned around and headed in the opposite direction. Luke smiled. Life had changed drastically in the week he'd been home. For the better. He wasn't fooling himself like some of the guys did. War was never good. He felt his own mortality weighing on him. If he didn't make it back, his mother and Rayanne would have Galen. He was a good man and would be there for both of them, and the baby. Of that Luke was sure.

The house was quiet when Luke got back. He'd taken his time on his walk and it was later than he'd planned to be out. Maybe it was just as well. Rayanne had tried to hide it, but he knew she was tired. He suspected that if not consciously, then sub-consciously, he had stayed out long enough for her to be asleep when he got back. He'd set it up himself, but this sham of a marriage was a lonely place to be. The unfurnished house made it seem even more lonely.

He took a beer he'd had sitting in an ice bucket and went out to the back porch. He rarely smoked, but nights like tonight he was glad he kept a few in the car. Lighting up, he sat on one step and leaned back against the one above him. It would be September soon. They had been told it would get cold overseas but right now with the balmy evening air it didn't seem real. Luke looked up at the sky, picking out some of the constellations. In a few weeks he would be looking at the same sky in a different country. A war-torn country. He didn't have the delusions about war that some did. He loved flying but not shooting and killing. From what he had been told the new flying machines, helicopters, would be primarily used for taking in supplies and bringing out the wounded. Something he could grab on to.

Luke was finally starting to get sleepy, though he wasn't looking forward to another night in back seat of the car. The noise of the back door softly opening made him turn to see Rayanne standing behind him. She had on a long night gown that he suspected would be revealing but for the blanket he recognized as the one on her bed wrapped around her. Without saying a word, she sat down beside him. Too close. His breath caught in his throat.

They sat there in silence listening to night sounds. Finally, Rayanne's whispered words reached out to him. "Come to bed. You have to be tired."

"I'm okay." His own voice sounded whiskey rough to him.

"Let me tell you a story," she whispered back.

When he nodded, she told him a history story about the practice of couples sharing a bed before marriage and the act of using a bundling board. "It was most popular in the eighteenth century and was used in British North American colonies as well as in Europe by Welsh, Dutch, and German peasants."

118

Luke didn't know what to say. Was she suggesting they do something like that? It would sure beat the hell out of the back seat of the car.

"Are you sure?" He swallowed. "Are you sure you trust me?"

Rayanne put her hand over his. "I'm positive."

She stood up and led the way back to the bedroom. Luke stopped by the bathroom, when he entered the room she was already in bed. She pulled back the top blanket for him. "We'll use the sheet for our bundling board." She chuckled.

Luke slid under the blanket leaving his pants on and let out a sigh of comfort. At base most of the men slept in their skivvies. Would the day ever come when he could again sleep attired in his preferred way, with nothing on? Rayanne's breathing leveled out. She was asleep. He swallowed the lump in his throat realizing that she really did trust him. Vowing he would hold that trust dear, he felt himself drift off to sleep too.

****

Rayanne had left the window open, and she woke up to the sounds of birds. The blanket that Luke had hung over the window darkened the room so like the day before, she couldn't tell what time it was. She hadn't been surprised to find Luke already up. She hoped he'd gotten a good night's sleep. She certainly had, making her doubly glad she had invited him to share the bed with her. They would get a sofa today so she could sleep on it, but being honest with herself, she liked sharing the bed better. Still, it wasn't fair to Luke. From what the women at the phone company talked about, men were different than women. If she hadn't been so tired last night, she doubted she would have gone to sleep as soon as she did. She'd certainly had trouble when Luke was out walking and was wide awake when he came back. Would her normal tossing and turning make Luke want more than they had agreed on? And if it did, would that be a bad thing?

"Good morning," Luke greeted her as she walked into the kitchen.

Being a new house there were no curtains at the windows and Rayanne visualized making some. They would be maybe white eyelet with yellow flowers if she could find material. She would make yellow place mats or a tablecloth to match when they got a kitchen table. She loved this house.

"It is a good morning. Luke, I love this house." She bit back the words on the tip of her tongue; *I think I love you too.*

"I'm glad. Let's take our coffee out to the back porch. I'll be glad when we have a table and chairs. We've been lucky with the weather, but you know Washington. It can rain a lot. The porch might work for now but you never know what the day will hold weather wise."

Rayanne laughed, a happy laugh. "The weather is only part of our luck. Or at least my luck." Her voice turned sober. "I wish you weren't going overseas."

"Do you really?" Luke turned away to pour the coffee.

"Yes," she whispered.

The air seemed to crackle with energy as Luke turned, locking his gaze with Rayanne's. She took a step toward him just as a rap sounded on the back door. "Mom's timing has to get better," Luke mumbled as he walked over and opened the door.

"I knew you two would be up. Another busy day for you." Luke's mom smiled.

Luke opened the door wider. "We were just having coffee out on the porch."

"I won't stay long, but I have something to tell you."

Luke didn't have to guess what it was. Galen must not have wasted any time after talking to him last night.

As soon as they were settled on the porch, Luke's mother almost blurted out her news. "Galen asked me to marry him."

Rayanne reached over and impulsively hugged Annie. "I am so happy for you." Smiling she added, "I'm not surprised. It isn't hard to see he loves you."

"You two should have gotten married years ago, mom," Luke said.

"Galen told me he'd talked to you."

"He did, last night, and you both have my blessing though you don't need it. I," Looking over at Rayanne he corrected himself, "*We*, are happy for you."

Rayanne surprised herself when she said, "Now our baby will have a grandfather."

Annie beamed. All three sat in silence while they savored the joy and peace surrounding them. Then Annie said, "I wish Galen could have heard you say that. Oh Rayanne, I am so happy. Everything would be perfect if only the war was over."

Luke hugged his mother. "It will be and soon. I'll be home before you know it."

Rayanne glanced over at him knowing that, like her, he was thinking about how their life would change yet again when he came home.

****

Rayanne couldn't make up her mind at the furniture store. There were two sofa's that she liked. Both had matching chairs. The trouble was that she really like the one chair and it was the most expensive set. "You sit in the chairs and tell me which one feels right for you," she told Luke.

"Honey, you're going to be the one living with it."

Honey. The word didn't go unnoticed by Rayanne, but she reminded herself that Luke was playing a role. "But if it's comfortable for you, it will be for Galen when they visit."

"There is that, I guess." Luke settled into the first chair, then switched to the second.

"I like this one," he said, pointing to the one Rayanne liked best.

"It costs more though," Rayanne countered.

The salesman cleared his throat. "I'll give you either set for the same price. You've bought a lot, so you deserve a price break."

"We'll take it." Luke smiled. By the time they had taken care of the paperwork and arranged for everything to be delivered the next morning, the day was pretty much gone.

"Let's get something to eat." Luke took Rayanne's arm as they left the furniture store. "Any place special you like?"

"I'd like to cook for you at least once before you leave. But we will need to stop at the grocery." Rayanne laughed. "You are beginning to make me think you're afraid of my cooking."

"Sounds good. We'll make like an old married couple tonight then."

At his words, Rayanne felt excitement.

Every minute she spent with Luke caused feelings she'd never had before. It's too soon, she reminded herself. They didn't know each other; she didn't know him. For one thing, he was almost too good to be true. Why hadn't he married before now? At twenty-eight most men were married and with families. Luke had said numerous times in the past days how ready he was for a family. So the question remained; Why was he still single? Oh, it was all so confusing. Why couldn't she just let everything unfold and enjoy her knight in shining armor and the perfect life he was affording her? Glancing over at Luke, her heart picked up its beat.

****

Luke had enjoyed dinner. Ham steak with creamy mashed potatoes and gravy were one of his favorite meals. "You are really a great cook. I could get used to dinners like this."

A blush spread across Rayanne's face. He'd bet she wasn't used to getting compliments and that was a shame. She was beautiful, but he'd noticed her reaction of disbelief when he told her. Not for the first time, he wondered about her life and how every day he learned new things about her.

"Let me help clear up." Luke picked up his plate.

"Oh, no. I can do it. I know you love to take a walk in the evenings. And the weather has been so beautiful."

"If I help, will you come with me?"

Rayanne looked at him in surprise. How could she not know he liked her company? They always found things to talk about. She was knowledgeable on a wide range of subjects and held her own in their debates. "Come on, you'll like going with me," he encouraged.

Laughing she agreed, and in short order they had the kitchen put to rights. Luke put his hand in the small of her back as they went through the front door. It felt good, like she belonged with him. At the curb he turned in the opposite direction from his mother's. The development was far from complete. Later there would be more houses, putting the one they had bought in about the middle of the complex. But for now, they were on the edge of a forest area.

He looked down at Rayanne. She looked so young. And, beautiful. "Promise to remember to keep your doors locked. Even though the depression is over there are still bums or hobo's that hang out in wooded areas."

Luke didn't want to scare her but he couldn't help but worry.

"I'll be okay. I grew up in the country and remember men coming to the door during the depression. They mostly were looking for work in exchange for food."

"I know, but things are changing and locking your doors is a good practice to get into."

Rayanne assured him she would. She added, "I will get acquainted with our neighbors too. Didn't Galen say there were other military wives in the neighborhood?"

"He did." Luke nodded. He was happy she'd mentioned it.

They got to the edge of the woods. There was a well-worn trail. It was narrow, forcing Rayanne to walk ahead. Luke liked that she had curves in all the right places. He forced his mind away from even thinking along those lines. They couldn't go too far in without a flashlight and in just a few minutes he said as much. "Let's go back and walk through a little more of the development."

"I wonder if there are blackberries," Rayanne said.

"I'd be surprised if there weren't. They grow all over the place," Luke answered.

"It's a little early for them to be ripe, which is too bad. I bake a good pie."

Luke laughed. "I'll hold that thought for when I come home."

For a few minutes neither said anything. Luke savored the feeling that this was a normal relationship and that there would be a home coming. In his mind he could see himself opening the door to a wife overjoyed to see him. She would be holding a baby girl with eyes like hers. A yearning growing from inside and spreading out made him draw in a deep breath. Bringing himself back to reality he led the way back to where lights from the few occupied homes shone out into the night.

When they got back to their house they opted to sit on the front porch where Luke had set a bench he'd purchased at the furniture store. It was handmade by a local craftsman and had caught his eye as a perfect piece for the porch.

"I'll run in and get us a glass of wine." Rayanne quickly disappeared.

Luke didn't stop her to say he'd prefer a beer. Wine would do for tonight. She'd been quiet on the walk back. Did she have any idea of the feelings he was struggling with or was the attraction one-sided? He would like to do what came naturally and find out, but then he would risk that she was submitting because she felt she owed him something. He didn't want submission, he wanted participation and passion.

****

Rayanne took her time getting the wine. She loved the little kitchen and easily got caught up in dreaming of how she would make it a home. Thankful that Luke was leaving her his car, she would drive out to her father's and see if she could get her sewing machine. The worst he could do was say "no." And, if she was at least partially ready for that, it wouldn't hurt too bad. But it could wait until Luke left. She didn't want him to see how her father felt about her. How he might treat her in front of Luke.

Walking out on the porch, she handed a glass to Luke and settled down beside him. "What is your favorite color?" Rayanne's eyes sparkled.

"Umm, I guess blue." Going along with Rayanne's excitement, Luke answered with a smile in his voice.

"Blue would be a good color."

"For anything specific?" Luke asked.

"I love this bench and thought maybe I'd make a cushion for it. I love a sunny yellow but it would be too light a color for outside."

"Sounds good. I'm glad you like the bench. And what you have planned for it makes me wish I could stick around for a few months and help you get the house set up."

Rayanne reflected on what he said. At first, she couldn't wait for Luke to go. Not to war but just not so close. Now having him around, especially at night, felt right. "I wish you could too," she answered honestly.

Luke turned toward her. The bench was about five feet long giving them plenty of room but not too much. "Do you?" His gaze found hers and in the dim light seemed to hold her spellbound.

Rayanne couldn't form words so instead nodded. She sat still, watching as Luke slowly lowered his mouth to hers. His lips tasted of blackberry wine. She relaxed, feeling like she could melt as warmth spread through her. He led the kiss while she followed. Slowly, softly until she felt his tongue. She opened her lips and he deepened the kiss. They were both still holding their wine glasses, impeding more than the kiss. When Luke broke away, Rayanne unconsciously made a whimper of protest.

"Shhh." Again, Luke held her gaze with his. Taking her glass from her hand he set it down on the floor beside him. Then took her into his arms.

Rayanne snuggled close. She wanted to melt into him, become one with him. His words pushed reality away.

"You make me want," he whispered.

"Me too," Rayanne whispered back.

"Are you sure?"

Rayanne closed her eyes and drew him closer to her. He didn't need more and picked her up.

Luke kicked the door shut behind them. The bedroom seemed further away than she remembered but it didn't take long to get there. Putting her down, he pulled back the covers. Then again took her in his arms. Standing tight against him, Rayanne could feel his need and her body softening to his touch. It hadn't been anything like this the first time. The first time they had made love she hadn't felt like this. Her heart was racing as his hands and lips moved over her. He reached between them to unbutton her blouse. She helped, then reached to help him with his clothes. When he hesitated for a second, she wanted to beg him not to stop.

His breath caught as he said, "we can slow down, we have all night."

She answered, "we'll slow down next time." Then couldn't believe it was her saying those words.

The chuckle escaping Luke assured her, and she laughed back as she initiated another kiss.

Chapter 10

The days sped by. Luke made time to put in some flower beds around the front porch. It was too late to plant much but there would be fall bulbs to plant for spring flowers and some bushes. Rayanne thought of the lilac and wondered where Luke would be when it bloomed. There weren't many minutes of the day that he didn't fill her thoughts. Days were filled with laughter and stolen bedroom play. Nights were intoxicating. Rayanne went on walks with Luke and they turned in as soon as the sun went down. Most nights with Luke bemoaning the still long days.

Luke was a patient lover, taking his time to bring her along with him. He was also a strong lover that let her unleash her own passion. Passion she'd never been aware she possessed.

It was Friday, the day Luke and his unit were scheduled to report back to base. Rayanne tried not to fully wake up. She didn't want it to be Friday. Finally opening her eyes, she looked directly into Luke's. "How long have you been awake and watching me?" she asked.

He smiled a slow, lazy smile. "Only for a few minutes. You're beautiful, your eye lashes are long and…"

Rayanne snuggled closer. Luke always got up before her and put coffee on. Not this morning, this, their last morning was different. They made slow perfect love and then lay silently in each other's arms. Neither voiced what was in their minds. For Rayanne, she wanted to tell him she loved him. But she had waited too long and she didn't want to send him off feeling obligated. Amber would have laughed and said Rayanne was mixing love up with sex. And, she probably was. She wasn't experienced in sex and had never been in love so how could she be sure? Then there was the fact that Luke said a lot of loving things, whispered them, but never the words "I love you."

"You're awfully quiet this morning." He gave her a quick peck on the lips and slid out of bed.

Rayanne didn't know what to say back so she let it go. Luke had arranged the day. He wanted to get up to the base around mid-day. They were going to swing by and pick-up Noah and Amber. It would give Rayanne someone to ride back with. His mother would have gone, but now he could say good-bye to her at home, which he preferred. If it wasn't that he was leaving the car for Rayanne, he would have no doubt driven himself up to the base.

With everything planned, Rayanne dressed carefully. She wanted Luke to remember her looking her prettiest. She liked to hear him say she was beautiful, but still had trouble believing him. She was just beginning to have a baby bump that didn't show in the full skirted sundress she'd chosen to wear. Not working nights had allowed her more sun time and she had managed a golden tan. She knew she looked healthier and happier than anytime she could remember. But did she look sexy? How did Luke see her?

They took their coffee out to "their" bench on the

front porch. Comfortable silence surrounded them. Luke broke it. "I'm going to miss this. I'm going to miss you."

She was going to miss him more, but she didn't say it out loud. "I'll write."

"Promise?"

"Cross my heart."

****

Noah had been staying with Amber, something that could have never happened at the old apartment. They were ready when Luke drove up. "Ready?" Luke called out of his open window.

"No?" Noah answered as he opened the trunk of the car to stow his bag.

Luke laughed. He wasn't ready either but doubted it would get any easier to leave. In fact, no doubt it would only get harder. Rayanne had chosen this morning to sit right next to him instead of sitting as far across the seat as she could. He'd been telling himself that he wasn't "in" love. He loved her, enjoyed—no *more than enjoyed*—the intimacy. He was continually surprised with his wife's passion. But in love? He had accepted that his one true love was flying. He had planned to make the air force his life, but lately he had been thinking about after the war. Peacetime would or could bring more flying challenges. No doubt the private sector would need pilots.

Noah made conversation from the back seat. "So, you are really going to leave your precious car with this lady?"

Luke chuckled, lightening his words. "This lady is my wife. And yes, it is all hers."

****

"I promised him I would take good care of it." Rayanne squeezed Luke's hand that rested on her leg.

Luke was still recovering from saying goodbye to his mother. Galen had been there. It was pretty obvious that he had all but moved in. Rayanne knew Luke felt relief that his mother had Galen. They had been friends for a long time. In fact, Anne had known Galen first. He had actually introduced her to Luke's father. As if reading her thoughts, Luke quietly said, "I don't know what took those two so long. They belong together."

Rayanne knew part of their story and again squeezed Luke's hand. She wished he could be at their wedding but Anne, after waiting for so many years wanted to have her church family witness it and there just hadn't been time. Besides she said she was torn about taking any time away from Luke and Rayanne.

"I'll send you pictures of the wedding," Rayanne promised. Luke had bought her a Brownie camera and Rayanne had already used half a roll of film. She loved it.

"You be sure to do that." He smiled over at her.

And then, they were at the guard house of McChord Field. Rayanne drew in her breath at the view before her. Mt. Rainier stood sentinel in the background. Two guards stood at the gate as cars stopped before driving through. The scene was somber but beautiful and peaceful. How could there be a war raging? Again, Luke seemed attuned to her. "It will be over before you know it."

He put the car into park. "We'll get out here and walk in." Opening his door, he moved to get out, then stopped. Turning to Rayanne, he drew her into his arms. What started out as an innocent chaste kiss quickly deepened. "Damn, I wish we had more time."

"I'll miss you," Rayanne stammered as she fought tears.

Both men slung their rucksacks over their shoulders and, with a final wave and a smile, they walked into base.

In a few minutes the men had cleared the gate. Rayanne watched them walk away without looking back. Still, she held back her tears just in case because she didn't want Luke to remember her crying.

Amber for once was silent as she wiped at tears coursing down her cheeks. "How can you be so strong?" She hiccupped. Rayanne put the car into gear, and with one last look at Luke's retreating back, pulled away from the air force field.

"You love Noah." It wasn't a question.

"I honestly don't know," Amber answered anyway. "I'll miss him, but Noah isn't a forever type of guy. I knew that going in."

"Do you have to work this afternoon?"

"Yeah, I do, and I'm glad. The last thing I want to do is hang around the apartment and going out would be uncouth, even for me." Amber flipped open her cigarette case and reached for the lighter.

Rayanne knew Luke didn't like smoking in the car and it would most likely make her sick, but she didn't have the heart to say anything. Instead, she rolled down her window.

"Sorry. I forgot about you getting sick." Amber rolled down her own window and stuck her hand with the cigarette out.

Amber's voice sounded wistful in the silence, except for the noise of the cool air flowing in from the windows, "It looks like you and Luke are doing okay."

"He's an amazing guy and really good to me."

"You could do worse."

Rayanne changed the subject. She was so close to tears. Holding them back she asked Amber how she liked the new apartment. They made small talk as they headed back from the base and were only a few blocks away from Ambers when her friend blurted out, "I'm late."

Rayanne, thinking she meant late for work, said, "Oh you still have plenty of time. It's only two o'clock or there abouts."

Amber shook her head. "I mean I'm late for my monthly."

Rayanne couldn't help the gasp that escaped. There was no reason to whisper, but she did. "It could just be the stress of moving and Noah leaving and…"

Amber looked over at her but didn't say a word. Finally, when the silence seemed to be choking them, Rayanne, with a low voice, asked, "How late?"

Amber took a deep drag from her second cigarette. "That's the good part. I'm only late by a couple of weeks."

"It could be—"

Before she could say more Amber interrupted. "No. I'm never late."

They pulled up in front of the apartment. "Would you like to come in?" Amber asked.

"I would, but you need to get ready for work. Maybe you can spend the day with me on your next one off."

It was apparent that both women were avoiding the elephant in the car. Rayanne wanted to ask Amber what she planned to do but doubted if she knew herself. They were leaving a lot unsaid and Rayanne didn't have a good feeling.

Amber got out of the car and thanked Rayanne, then turned toward the apartments. "Wait." Rayanne turned off the car and got out. "Don't do anything until we talk more."

Amber looked lost for a second and then put on her tough face. "I shouldn't have said anything. You know me. I can take care of myself." She shrugged. "Besides it really might be nothing."

"When is your next day off?"

"I won't be getting one for a while. I need to pay back the extra ones I took to be with Noah."

Relief settled over Rayanne. If Amber had to work, she wouldn't be doing anything foolish. Rayanne didn't even want to think what that might be.

The ride home took her through places where it looked like she could reach out and almost touch Mt. Rainier. The scene pulled her mind off of what Amber had said. Or at least for the moment. She enjoyed driving, but she missed Luke. More than she could believe. The day stretched out in front of her and she decided to stop off and see if Annie was home. Luke's mother had to be feeling some of what she was.

She hadn't been there very long before Galen came in the back door. "Hey girl, just the person I wanted to see. Did you get our guy off okay?"

Rayanne laughed. Galen looked so at home here. She wondered if the couple would stay here after they were married or maybe move into one of the new homes he was building. "I did. It was sad and Amber cried."

"You didn't?" Galen teased.

"Well, maybe just a little."

"Seriously, I did want to see you. I have a refrigerator for you."

"Oh." Luke had been worried that he hadn't had time to get one. She had tried to tell him she could make do with an ice box but he had been still fussing about it this morning.

"I have it in the truck. Annie and I can bring it down later."

"We can do it now if you have time," Rayanne said.

It didn't take long to get the fridge in the house. Annie hugged Rayanne as they were leaving. "I'll see you tomorrow and you can tell me what's bothering you. Besides Luke leaving that is."

Rayanne laughed and agreed. Had she been so transparent, or was she more worried about Amber than she thought? She'd never had a confidante before and had learned to keep things to herself. Now she worried if she had the right to share Amber's condition. Rayanne had no doubt that she could trust Luke's mother but even with best intentions things could slip out. Look what had happened with the news of her own coming baby.

The house felt empty when Galen and Luke's mother left. Rayanne had never lived by herself. The apartment she had shared with Amber was as close to being by herself as she had been. A new chapter she thought as she locked the door. She wouldn't be walking tonight. Not by herself.

All at once, like a flood gate, the tears she had been holding at bay let loose and Rayanne sobbed like there was no tomorrow. She loved Luke. It wasn't a question any longer; it was a hard fact. "Please bring him home," she whispered into the darkening room.

****

Rayanne hadn't slept well. Or at least not until the first light of day peeked around the blanket at the window. Then she went out so hard that now her head felt like a drum was beating in it. She pushed back the blanket and made her way to the bathroom. The mirror over the sink confirmed that it hadn't been a good night.

Finishing her morning ablutions quickly, she put her toothbrush away, fingering the cup that just yesterday had held two toothbrushes. "Well, of course his is gone," she mumbled to herself as she made her way back to the bedroom to dress. One of the things Luke had put on the list he had made for her, was to get a phone. Beside the notation he had scribbled, *I won't be able to call you until you do.* If he thought that would tempt her to get one, he thought right. In a few minutes she had coffee perking and was starting a new list for herself.

1. Get a phone

2. See about getting my sewing machine.

With the coffee done she took her cup out to the front porch. The bench seemed bigger without Luke sharing it with her. The morning was cool, but promised another warm day. She would need a hose to water the small patch of lawn and the lilac bush. No matter what she couldn't let it die. If Luke wasn't home by the time it bloomed, she would snip a piece of a blossom and send it to him in a letter. The smell of home, he had said, and Rayanne wanted more than anything for him to think of this as his home.

When she returned inside, she glanced at the clock and noted the time. It was still early and she dreaded the long day ahead of her. The house was clean but she whisked through it anyway. The small yard didn't need anything either but like the house she walked around plucking the few weeds that had poked up. Without Luke everything felt strange and she kept thinking she was forgetting something. The only thing she had really accomplished was to start a letter to Luke.

Since it was Saturday and the business office was closed, she would have to wait a couple of days to call the phone company. Which brought up the fact that since it was Saturday her father wouldn't be at work. Still, if she wanted to catch him at home, it was safer to wait until the next day. For sure he wouldn't be in church. Or maybe even better to wait for a few weeks just in case the visit didn't go well. At least by waiting she would be more used to living alone.

At loose ends with nothing to do, she smiled when she heard Annie at the door. Welcoming her in Rayanne offered sweet tea. "I have sun tea sitting outside but it isn't ready yet so we'll have to make do with this," Rayanne said as she poured a cup and handed it to Annie.

"How are you doing?" Annie asked as she settled herself at the kitchen table.

"Okay. The day has been long without Luke. He likes to walk in the evenings and mornings but I didn't go out last night or this morning."

"It will get better as you settle in." Annie reached down for her bag and drew out a book. "*A Tree Grows In Brookland*, I got it at the library and thought you might like to read it. I enjoyed it."

"Oh, thank you so much. I love reading and when I return this book, I can get a library card. I should have thought about this myself. When I was in town and working, I never had much time. But I used to read a lot at home."

"I don't drive so when you take it back let me know and maybe I can go with you."

"Do you have something now? Because if not I can take you Monday."

"No, just when you're ready. I still have a couple from my last trip. The bus goes right by the library if you don't want to use your gas rations." Annie settled back before looking at Rayanne. "Was it hard for you to say good-bye to Luke yesterday?"

Rayanne nodded. "Harder than I could have believed, but it was worse coming home without him. The house seemed bigger and so empty."

Annie patted Rayanne's hand. "Luke's father was in the military though he wasn't a career man. And, thankfully, he wasn't in any battles, but he was gone a lot. I know from experience that it will be easier when the baby comes. They can keep you unbelievably busy for such wee little things."

Rayanne laughed. "I don't have any brothers or sisters and haven't been around little kids let alone babies. I have so much to learn."

"It all comes naturally so don't worry and I hope you'll let me help. I've wanted a grandbaby for so long." Her voice sounded wistful. "I had all but given up getting one." She laughed. "Or two. Do twins run in your family?"

Rayanne joined her in laughing. "I don't know, but

I hope there aren't two. Luke won't want to come home."

She told Annie that she was going to call and see about getting a phone on Monday and Annie agreed she needed one, adding, "this party line is really something. I swear the minute you pick up the receiver half a dozen women are listening in."

"So, if I needed help, all I would have to do is pick the phone up and holler?"

"Probably, but if you need help you better call me." Annie paused. "I will always be here for you and the baby."

Rayanne felt tears spring up. Her life had changed so much in two weeks. A husband and a bonus of having a "real" mother, one who cared about more than herself. "Thank you," she whispered.

Annie stayed for over an hour and by the time she left Rayanne was feeling so much better. Deciding that if she walked early enough it would be safe, she accompanied Annie part way to her house before parting to continue alone. The day hadn't gotten as hot as she thought it might be and there was a refreshing breeze. By the time she got back home she was hungry, something that didn't happen often.

The evening passed quickly with the book Annie had brought. Adding the library to her list, Rayanne got ready for bed and immediately started thinking of Amber. She didn't know when Amber would get a day off. Would she try to terminate the pregnancy? Amber had talked about it when she found out Rayanne was pregnant. She had said something about doing it right away because the further along you were the more dangerous it was. Rayanne shuddered as questions filled her mind. Like, would Amber tell Noah? Could she go home to her parents or the sister Rayanne knew she had? Making a note in her head to call Amber as soon as she had a phone, Rayanne closed her eyes.

It took a few days but soon things eventually fell into a routine. Rayanne would tidy the house in the mornings and then if the weather permitted take a walk. By the time she got back it was time to fix something for lunch and then a nap which she had never indulged in before. She always finished her day with writing to Luke.

Tonight, she would finish the current letter and mail it off. Then start the next one. She had thought she would try to send a letter a week but had found she was a little to prolific so better to just send them when she had three or four pages.

It had been a week since Luke left, and the second weekend without him loomed.

The phone rang, startling Rayanne. She still wasn't used to having her very own phone. Friday night, who would be calling? With the anticipation of a kid on Christmas morning, Rayanne picked up the receiver. When she heard Luke's voice her heart raced.

"Hi." He sounded like he was in the same room with her.

"You sound so close."

Luke laughed. "Ahh the wonders of modern technology. How have you been?"

"Oh Luke, I love this house. I love your mother." She paused and blurted out, "I lo—*miss,* you."

If Luke noticed her nearly saying "love," he ignored it. "I miss you too," Not pausing he continued on, "I see you got the phone in. I was really happy when mom gave me the number."

She had so many questions. Like where was he at? Was he still at the base? How was the food? But Rayanne was very conscious of the cost of a long-distance call so they didn't talk long. When she hung up it was like when she had come home after dropping Luke off at the base, the house felt strangely like it had grown and it was so quiet. Rayanne stepped outside in the growing dusk and sat on the bench—*their* bench. Her hand rested on the spot where Luke always sat. She could almost feel his warmth there. Hugging herself, she wished it were Luke's arms around her.

The next morning Rayanne hurried back from her walk. She was going to the library today and was excited about getting a library card. She had asked Annie to go but her mother-in-law had plans for the day. Rayanne would have loved the company but this way she would drive on into Olympia and see Amber. Maybe even splurge and go get something to eat. She pondered calling Amber before starting out but then decided to just surprise her. Like her mother-in-law had cautioned, the phone party-line was very active. It wouldn't do to let something slip out regarding Amber's condition. Or hers either.

Rayanne had been in the library almost two hours when she noticed the time. As she walked out the door with her book selections she vowed to be back soon. Then thinking back to her conversation with Luke the night before she silently laughed at herself. *I think I am in love with my world.*

A few minutes later she was knocking on Amber's door, and was relieved to hear someone on the other side. The door opened a crack and a disheveled looking

Amber peeked out. Seeing Rayanne, she swung the door open. "Come in, excuse the mess you know how swing shift is." Then laughing she continued, "Who am I kidding? I'm a slob. It was always you who kept our place up. And motivated me to do the same."

"I thought maybe you would like to run out for a bite to eat. Do you have to work tonight?"

Amber laughed and at once looked better. "First, I would love to go out. Second, I do have to work but this is an extra shift so I don't go in until eight o'clock."

"Wow, that's late. Is it for only four hours?"

"You got it. Why don't you make yourself a cup of coffee while I get dressed? Betty stayed overnight with a friend so she might not even come home today."

Rayanne was ready for a cup of coffee but tea sounded better. She made her way to the kitchen and put on some hot water. Like the living room, the kitchen was a mess. Dishes from what looked like a few days sat in the sink and the counters were cluttered. Rayanne sighed. *Somethings never change.* Amber wasn't a home maker that was for sure. Not for the first time Rayanne wondered how her friend was going to manage.

It didn't take long for Amber to get ready. For one thing, Rayanne had never seen her with so little make-up on. Freckles sprinkled over her nose making her look younger, and more vulnerable. They opted for the little café a few blocks away and decided to walk down.

"I have a phone now. Remind me to give you the number when we get seated," Rayanne said.

They went on with small talk until they placed their orders. Then Amber opened up the subject that seemed to be sitting in the booth with them. "I'm getting a little of the morning sickness you had. Who would have guessed it with old iron stomach here?"

"Oh, I hope it isn't as bad as mine. Are you managing at work, at least better than I did?"

"Yes, I think yours was extreme. Mine is just when I first wake up. I'm glad I don't have the morning shift." Amber sobered. Her voice sounded sad and resigned. "I have an appointment for tomorrow."

"On a Sunday?" Rayanne asked.

Amber nodded. "They say it's an easy procedure and I will be fine in a day, so since I don't work on Sunday…" She shrugged as if to blow the whole thing off.

She didn't have to spell out what the appointment was for. Rayanne knew at once. She unconsciously placed a protective hand over her baby bump. Rayanne's heart hurt for Amber. Even though she was putting up a good front, Rayanne could see that it was only a front. From the look on her face, she knew Amber didn't want to do this.

"Could you go home to your parents or sister instead?" Rayanne asked.

"I could… but with the economy what it is my parents are struggling."

"June, your sister, then?"

Amber looked down at the table. "I was going to tell June. Not to ask her to take me in but to go with me to… *you know*."

"Are you sure?"

She sighed, looking down at the table between them. "It's murder. At least to my family and I guess me. I'll have to live with it… but they are all innocent and I decided that the less who know, the better. I probably shouldn't have told you."

"I'm glad you did. You shouldn't be doing this all by yourself. Let me take you to your appointment tomorrow."

A tear slid down Amber's cheek. "Would you?"

Rayanne reached over and took Amber's hand. "Of course I will, but have you really thought about your options? You know it hasn't been long since we were laying out mine."

"I remember," Amber whispered.

"So, what about adoption?"

Amber shook her head.

Rayanne took a breath and asked the question she had been holding back. "Have you told Noah? And, if not, are you going too?"

"It isn't the same for me as it was for you and Luke. I knew the score going in with Noah. I haven't told him and I for sure won't tell him about the…" She looked away avoiding even voicing the word.

Rayanne felt tears well up inside her. Forcing them back, knowing she needed to be strong for Amber, she whispered. "What time do you want me to pick you up?"

The food arrived but neither of the women were as hungry as they thought. Finally, Rayanne took charge and requested a carry out bag. A few minutes later they were outside in the fresh air. Amber took a breath. "Thank you."

"You bet. So, you didn't tell me what time."

Amber chuckled. "I don't know what's wrong with me. This shouldn't be affecting my brain but it sure seems like it is. The appointment is for one thirty, but I'm not sure exactly where it is so we should probably leave here around noon."

Rayanne hugged Amber at her door and assured her she would see her the next day. As soon as Rayanne got into the car she started shaking. In some ways this seemed worse than when she had first learned she was pregnant and had considered terminating it. Back then Amber had seemed so—*worldly*. Like she had all the answers. Now she looked like what she was, a very scared young woman all on her own. Did it have to be this way? Would Noah step up to the plate like Luke had done? The memory of her own home life with parents that hated each other flashed through her mind. For the first time she wondered if her mom and dad had thought about terminating the pregnancy. If they had, she wouldn't be here. She pressed a hand to her stomach as the realization that the little life inside wouldn't be either. Love for the baby and Luke filled her heart.

In an instant she whipped on to a side street and turned around. She would offer Amber an alternative. She already owed Luke so much, what was more debt? She would pay it all back to him, it would just take longer.

Chapter 11

It took Amber a bit to come to the door. When she did, she looked like she had been crying. Rayanne didn't wait to be invited in. Instead, she just pushed the door a little wider and went on in.

Amber wiped her face. "Did you forget something? Or change your mind about going with me tomorrow?"

Rayanne stepped closer giving Amber a hug. "Of course not. I have a plan I want to tell you about."

"If you're going to try to talk me out of…"

Rayanne wasn't surprised Amber struggled with the word "abortion" or even termination. "No, I know how hard this is and I don't want to make it harder. If you do this, I'll never judge. Instead, I'll just be here for you."

That did it. Amber started sobbing. Not what Rayanne had intended at all. At the rate things were going Amber would never make it to work today.

"Shhh." Rayanne took Amber by the hand and walked her over to the couch. Leaving her for a minute, she went into the kitchen and brought back a glass of water. "Here, try to drink this and let me tell you my plan."

Amber composed herself and again dried her face. Blowing her nose, she nodded for Rayanne to continue.

"First, don't worry about making any decision. Instead, it will be something to think about as an alternative to tomorrow."

Rayanne didn't try to find the right words and instead just blurted out, "You can come stay with me." Immediately Amber started shaking her head.

"Like I said, it's something to think about. The house has two bedrooms. I know you need to live here while you can work, but after that you can move down to my place. You won't have rent and I'll take care of groceries. Then after the baby comes, if you choose to keep it, you can probably get a job at the Purcy phone company and I can babysit for you."

Amber was still shaking her head. "Babies cost money and I'm not very good with money. You know that. How many times have I had to borrow from you to get to the next paycheck?"

"I'll help you. Luke was right in that marrying him gave me military benefits."

Amber opened her mouth, but before she could say anything Rayanne went on. "I'm keeping track of everything Luke pays out of his pocket, and I intend to pay him back." Still not giving Amber a chance to say no, Rayanne stood up and moved to the door. "Like I said, think about it. I'll be here by noon tomorrow. Either way, we'll need to talk in person as we for sure can't say a thing over the phone."

Back in the car, Rayanne drove home slowly. She had a lot to think about herself, including one thing that she hadn't counted on. The big "if." If her mother and father had terminated the pregnancy that changed and ruined their lives, she wouldn't be here. She was ready to put a visit to her father on the top of her list of things to-do.

Rayanne couldn't settle down to the book she was

reading that night. She kept thinking about Amber. Finally giving up she went to bed and that didn't turn out to be any better. The last time she'd looked at the clock it was three in the morning. "Oh boy, I'm going to look a fright in the morning," she mumbled to herself.

She finally fell asleep and slept so soundly she woke up late. She put on water for tea since coffee could still be iffy for her stomach and went to get dressed for the day. Again, her thoughts went to Amber. Would she take her up on the offer or go through with the appointment? Rayanne always closed her day writing to Luke but last night, fearing she'd let something slip out, she had made an exception. She wanted so badly to share what she had proposed to Amber but it wasn't her story to tell. Still, if she did, would he tell Noah? And, would Noah take at least some responsibility? She wasn't under any illusions that he would take over like Luke had done, and she knew Amber didn't expect it either.

The morning whizzed past and Rayanne tried hard not to think of what lay ahead of Amber if she decided to keep the appointment. As Rayanne drove to Olympia, she tried to think positive and set worry aside.

Amber was ready and waiting for her. Without saying anything, it was apparent that Amber had decided to go through with the procedure. Rayanne was disappointed, but she'd been talking to herself about not butting in. The offer to help was enough. The decision would change Amber's life, and it was hers to make. Biting back the words that threatened to escape, Rayanne put on a stoic, if not happy, face and waited for Amber to say something.

The other woman slipped into a sweater and grabbed her purse. "When I talked to the doctor, he insisted on cash. Strange but I talked to him, not a nurse, and he was very specific. He said fifty dollars in an envelope with no name or anything on the outside."

"Sort of sounds like one of those dark suspense books." Rayanne tried to smile. Wow, fifty dollars was a lot. "Do you have the money?" Amber lived each day as it came, and Rayanne was a bit surprised that her friend had saved that much.

Amber looked embarrassed. "Noah gave it to me that last day. When we were at the base, he handed me an envelope and told me not to open it for a month." She smiled. "Of course, I opened it as soon as I got home."

Amber handed her a slip of paper. Rayanne glanced down at it. She had lived around Olympia her whole life and she didn't recognize the address written on it. "Did he, the doctor, give you an idea of where this is?"

"I asked him. He said it was close to Tacoma. I wrote down the directions."

Both women were silent on the drive. When they turned off a side road Rayanne said, "This isn't a good neighborhood, Amber. It doesn't look like a place a doctor's office would be."

Amber looked as scared as Rayanne felt. A residential area had given way to a gravel road with deep potholes in it. As they bumped down the road, they could see a few houses far back from the road and none looked like much more than shacks. Rayanne held her breath praying that Amber would tell her to turn around, that she'd changed her mind.

Rayanne slowed for yet another deep rut at the same time that Amber pointed out the window. "There. The doctor said there was a red ribbon tied to a mailbox."

The lane looked like it hadn't been traveled a lot. It was narrow and berry bushes along the side of the road brushed against the car making Rayanne's fear ramp up. What was Amber thinking? Rayanne took a quick look over at her friend.

Amber sat ramrod straight in her seat. Her hands were clenched tight in her lap and it looked like a touch would shatter her.

"We... you, don't have to do this."

"I've thought and thought about it, Rayanne, and I know this is for the best. I knew we were taking risks. Or at least I was."

"Did you and Noah ever talk about the possibility of a baby?"

Amber gave a shaky non-chuckle. "You know Noah. He wasn't much for talking."

Rayanne really didn't know him all that well. She knew he could dance and liked a good time. He was funny, most of the time entertaining them. He was bad-boy handsome, and much to Amber's worry, women gravitated to him.

The car continued the slow bumpy drive until finally they reached the end. The house didn't look like it had ever seen a coat of paint. The porch reached all the way across the front but pieces of a railing were missing and the steps sagged. Worse, it looked dirty.

Before Rayanne could say anything, Amber opened her door and stepped out. Leaning back in the open door she said, "The doctor said not to bring anyone in with me."

"He would know you'd need a ride."

Before Rayanne could object and argue, Amber shook her head. "Stay here and wait for me. I don't think this takes long."

Rayanne watched as Amber trudged toward the steps of the house, then slowly made it up the stairs. When she got to the door, it opened before she could knock and then Amber was gone. As far out as this place was Rayanne wondered how Amber had planned to get out here. But then this was typical of Amber who never planned or thought a lot about the details.

It had rained hard the night before and the cold damp seemed to seep from the car into her bones as Rayanne sat huddled in her seat. She looked at the cheap little watch she had treated herself to. Today it wasn't the luxury she first thought it was, but instead an essential.

Twenty minutes passed. Rayanne felt fear creep over her as she imagined what might be happening inside the house. Even with the cold, she was sweating. What was it like for Amber? How long would they keep her after the procedure? For the first time Rayanne "really" looked at her surroundings. They were far enough off the road that her car couldn't be seen from it. This was horrible. Even if Amber came through this, what about infection? Nothing about this place looked clean. Rayanne could see an outhouse, so they didn't even have indoor plumbing. Her parents place hadn't had it until her mother had gotten really sick.

She looked at her watch again. Twenty-six minutes. It seemed closer to an hour. "This is crazy," Rayanne mumbled to herself. Something like this and time to recover enough to walk would take at least an hour.

Just as the thought passed her mind she saw the door to the house slowly open. Amber stood there for a second. She looked confused and uncertain. Rayanne didn't wait, instead, she fairly flew out of the car and ran toward the steps. Seeing her seemed to snap Amber out of it and she held up her hand. "I'm okay."

Without another word, both women hurried to the car. The yard provided space for Rayanne to thankfully turn the car. Backing out that long drive would have been a nightmare. By the time they had bumped and scraped their way back to the road Rayanne was shaking. Only too glad to have Amber, and heading away from that house, she took a deep breath. "How are you? Is the pain horrible?"

Amber shook her head. "I'm okay. Let's get back to a main road and I'll tell you all about it."

Amber looked better than Rayanne imagined she would, but she was still horribly pale. Rayanne repeated her earlier question. "Are you in a lot of pain?"

"I didn't go through with it."

Amber's voice was so low Rayanne wasn't sure she'd heard right. She waited for Amber to continue. It took what seemed like forever before Amber said, "It was so dirty, and I was so scared." Then like a floodgate had opened, the words spilled out of her. "The main room, what was probably a living room when it was a house had a worn, dirty sofa and a couple of kitchen chairs. The man, I don't think he is a doctor, wasn't even clean looking. He did have on a doctor's coat, but it was a dingy white. It didn't have any stains on it, but again, it didn't look clean. He told me to follow him and we went down a hall past a kitchen."

Amber stopped and looked over at Rayanne. "You should have seen the kitchen. Dirty dishes were everywhere and it smelled horrible. The bedroom wasn't even set up like a doctors would be. There was a twin bed that was on a raised platform. It was draped with a dingy sheet and there were horrible looking instruments on a stand next to it."

Rayanne felt like she was going to be sick. If *she* felt this way how was Amber doing? Taking a breath, she told herself this wasn't about her. "What did he say when you told him you couldn't do it?"

"Your choice missy. That's what he said."

"Had you given him the money?"

"Oh yeah. It was the first thing he said. Like, 'do you have it?'"

"Did he give it back to you?"

Amber shook her head. "He said if I changed my mind to call for another appointment."

Silence filled the car as they drove back on the country road. Finally, Rayanne asked, "Wasn't there a nurse?"

Amber let out a sort of snort. "No, only the man."

"Do you think you should report him to the police?"

Amber looked over at her as if she was crazy. "It's against the law to have an abortion. And, *he* warned me about that. He said if he was caught, he would make sure the authorities would have my name."

Rayanne gasped. "What a horrible man."

"Besides, I got the impression that he doesn't stay long in one place. As dirty as it was, it had a sort of empty abandoned look. I'm betting he moves around."

Rayanne didn't want to ask Amber what she was going to do. She doubted Amber even knew. They rode in silence for a while. Just before they got to the road that would take them to her house Rayanne said, "How about spending the night with me. You don't have to work tonight and I can take you home in the morning."

Rayanne hadn't thought Amber would take her up on her offer and was surprised when she nodded.

****

Rayanne picked up the phone to call Amber. It had been a week since she had talked to her friend. After the doctor's visit they had, by mutual silence, kept their conversation light and the issue at hand on the back burner. It had been late afternoon by the time they had gotten back to Rayanne's for dinner, after which both went to bed to read. Amber had told Rayanne the next morning that she'd had the best sleep she'd had in weeks.

The phone rang a couple of times before Amber picked it up.

"Did I wake you?" Rayanne asked.

"No but almost. I worked a half a shift over last night."

"Oh, is tonight a night off?"

"It would be, but Darlene is letting me take her shift."

Rayanne didn't need to ask why. "Let me know when your next day off is and I'll come over for a visit or pick you up and you can come out here."

They talked for a few more minutes, being careful of what they said over the party line. When Rayanne hung up, she found herself at loose ends. Living alone had some perks but mostly it was lonely. If she had a job, or a husband at home, it would be different. At that thought she made herself face reality. Her life wasn't going to be any fairytale but Annie, Luke's mother, had managed and so would she. And, it for sure could be worse. She could be in the same situation Amber was in. In fact, she was, initially. Without Luke's intervention she'd have been a lot worse off. Amber had her sister and hopefully her parents. Thinking of parents, Rayanne made a decision she'd been putting off. She had time today; she would go visit her father. She really needed her sewing machine and this afternoon was as good a time as any.

It took almost an hour to get to Highway 99 and then, to the west side of Olympia, but Rayanne enjoyed the ride. She found she liked driving, and would do more except for the gas rationing. She hadn't been out to her father's place since she'd left. She'd been close to going a couple of times but always found a reason to put it off. He hadn't tried to get a hold of her either.

Guilt mixed with worry on how her father would greet her overwhelmed her as she turned into the drive. His truck was parked on the side in front of a new garage. The place looked different, more cared for. Maybe her father had sold it? She parked the car and got out just as the front door opened. He stood in the doorway waiting for her to get out of the car.

"Hi dad." Rayanne felt tongue tied. In that moment she knew she hadn't been expecting him to be home. Foolish, as she shouldn't be wasting petrol. What did she say now? She searched for words, but he saved her the trouble.

"It's been a while. How's the job going?" He was reserved but not unfriendly.

Oh, boy. "The job? I have a lot to tell you," Rayanne stammered.

"Well come on in. I just put on some tea and there's ice, though it won't be long before we'll be wanting hot tea for the weather."

Rayanne couldn't believe what she was hearing. She wasn't sure what she had expected but it wasn't this. Her father actually sounded like he might be glad to see her. And tea?

He held the door open for her. The house smelled different: fresh and clean. For one thing it had been painted, no doubt some of the scent was because of that. And the windows were open, letting fresh air flow freely through. "The house looks great, dad."

"Yeah, should have done something with it before but your mom never wanted me to make a mess."

Really, that wasn't how Rayanne remembered things, but she didn't say anything and instead followed him into a sparkling kitchen.

"Sit down. This will only take a second. If I remember right you take sugar in your iced tea?"

Rayanne nodded. That he knew how she took her tea was another strange thing. Her father didn't sound nervous but she noticed that his hands shook when he took the sugar bowl out of the cupboard. A few minutes and her father put a glass of tea on the table and pushed the sugar bowl over to her. "Nice car. I'm glad to see you have wheels. This country isn't made to live without a car or truck. Not like New York where there is public transportation."

New York. Rayanne hadn't thought her father had gone further than from the house to the docks where he worked. She had so much to tell him but instead asked,

"You've been to New York?"

"There's a lot you don't know about me. I wasn't there long but it's not a city you forget. I imagine it's a lot bigger now." His voice sounded sad. "We really don't know each other, do we?"

Rayanne played with the moisture on her glass. "I guess not."

They sat in silence for a bit. Surprisingly it wasn't uncomfortable. Rayanne sipped her tea and finally broke the silence blurting out, "I'm married and I'm going to have a baby. I'm not working."

Her father swallowed a large gulp of tea. "Do you need help?"

"What? No."

His instant offer to help her surprised Rayanne back into silence for a second or two. "Thanks dad. I guess I wasn't expecting you to offer like this," she finally said.

Her father's face reflected pain at her words. "No, I don't expect you did. I haven't been much of a father. Hell, I haven't been a father at all." He reached over and put his hand over hers. Giving her a shaky smile, he asked her to tell him about her husband.

Later that evening, Rayanne got up to put their cups in the sink. Dusk was settling in and she didn't want to drive home in the dark. Or for that matter go into a dark house. She had found that her father was a good listener. Easy to talk too. How had she missed this all those years?

She turned back to her father. "Wow, I can't believe the time. I need to get going."

"I'm so glad you came. And so happy for you. Luke Accardo sounds like a good man. Let's hope this turns out to be a forever marriage, but if it doesn't you will always have a home with me."

It surprised Rayanne that she had told her father pretty much everything. Not at first, it had taken almost two hours but her father had participated with bits and pieces of his own life with her mother.

"It's getting chilly out, let me get you a jacket." Her father disappeared coming back with a sweater she had left in her old room. He handed it to her. "Everything is still like you left it."

The intent of the visit had been to see if her father would let her take her sewing machine but she didn't want to take anything away from the visit they'd had, so she decided to wait for another time.

Her father reached for the pad and pencil laying on the counter. "Give me your phone number. You still have mine?"

"I do." Rayanne wrote hers on the front of the pad.

Her father walked her out to the car, seemingly reluctant to see her go. "I'd like to take you to dinner. I could follow you into town."

Rayanne opened her car door and turned back, giving him a hug. "I'd love to but I really hate driving in the dark. Maybe next time."

Her father's face lit up with a smile. "Next time, for sure. That would be swell." He hugged her back.

Rayanne didn't want to leave him. It was so different from all the years growing up here. She started the car and rolled down her window for one last good-bye.

"Like I said, your old room is as you left it. With the baby coming and all, would you like to have your sewing machine? I mean I could bring it to you in the truck…"

"Oh dad, thank you. I would love to have it."

They talked about when would be a good time and decided the next day being Sunday would work. As Rayanne drove off, she glanced in the review mirror to see her father waving good-bye. Tears coursed down her face. She had a father and she was going to hang on tight to him.

Chapter 12

Rayanne woke early, and by the time her father pulled up to her house she had a black berry pie cooling, as well as a casserole in the oven. The night before she had spent almost an hour writing to Luke. She missed his phone calls though there hadn't been that many calls before he'd shipped out for England, the first leg of his journey into war. She would have liked to tell him about her father and their visit instead of writing to him about it. The letter, stamped and ready, sat on the counter ready for Monday's mail.

She rushed to open the door for her father. As soon as he got in the house, he gave her a hug. It seemed the most natural thing in the world. A miracle had happened the day before.

"Wow, it smells like a piece of heaven in here."

Rayanne felt the blush that she knew was lighting her face. The day was full of sunshine and not just from the weather. "Let me show you the house. It isn't very big, but perfect, and I so love it."

Her father complimented the layout and furnishings. "You have made it a home. Where would you like to put the sewing machine?"

"I thought about the nursery, but I know I'll need to use it when the baby is asleep so how about up against this wall." She pointed to a spot in the kitchen behind the table.

"Looks good. You could use the top when you have the cover on it."

Decided, they went out to get the machine. As they stepped out of the door Galen and Luke's mother came up the walk. Rayanne introduced them thinking how much she wished Luke were here. She had been doing that more and more. She wrote every day, but hadn't heard from him yet. Every day when the mail came with nothing, it took her a bit to get over the disappointment. Shaking off the melancholy, she smiled at Galen. "Your timing is perfect. Are you up to helping unload my sewing machine?"

"You betcha, sugar."

Galen and Rayanne had fallen into a comfortable friendship, often kidding around. If her father noticed he didn't show it. It would take them time to develop their relationship, though now, she had no doubt that they would.

Galen and her father hit it off almost immediately and she learned her father had wanted to be an architect when he was younger. She listened as he talked about the scholarship he'd planned to use for college.

"So, what happened?" Galen asked.

Her father shrugged. "Life. I joined the military. You know what they say, 'man plans, and God laughs.'"

Luke's mom and Rayanne left the men to their talk and drifted off to discuss the sewing she wanted to do. "First thing is curtains or maybe drapes so I won't need to hang blankets up at the windows at night. I feel so exposed if I don't put them up."

"Let me know if you need help. If not with the sewing, maybe when you get ready to hang them."

162

The afternoon passed quickly and Rayanne invited Galen and Annie to stay for dinner. They readily agreed saying the aroma wouldn't let them say no. Rayanne enjoyed every minute, but found she missed Luke more than when she was alone. She needed to get over it. This marriage, as perfect as it seemed in that short week together, wasn't real. Reminding herself of this caused her to catch her breath as emotion washed over her.

Dusk was falling when Rayanne and her father walked Galen and Annie out. "I need to get going too. Dinner was beyond great." Her father looked happy.

Smiling he said, "How about next weekend? Maybe you could come over Saturday and I'll take you out to dinner." When she hesitated, he continued, "Or I could give you a call maybe Friday."

"I want to come over, but I have a friend that I need to check in with and I'm not sure what day she has off from work. Could I maybe call you?"

"Sure, or bring her with you."

Rayanne had never been allowed to have friends over to her house when she was growing up. She had always thought it was because of her father, now she wasn't as sure. Before she could stop them, words flowed out in the form of questions. "Why didn't you ever want me to have friends over when I was growing up?"

They were standing by her father's car and he opened the door to sit down. "Is that what your mother told you?"

"Noooo, I just thought…"

"You thought wrong. Your mother told me that you were shy and didn't make friends like most girls." Her father shook his head. "Not that I paid all that much attention. I was a horrible father. I knew it then and I know it now."

After talking with her father the day before, Rayanne had guessed that all wasn't what was on the surface at her house all those years. She leaned up against the side of the car. "You know dad, maybe we should let the past go. We can't change it."

"I'd like that, but I think I am always going to regret those years."

Rayanne squatted down in front of his open door. "We have a baby coming and you are going to be the best grandfather ever. I read somewhere that everything that happens in our life, good, bad, and in between makes the person we are today. The person we are at this very minute. And, I like who you are." She lowered her voice to almost a whisper. "I hope you like who I am."

Her father was out of the car in a flash pulling her to her feet and into his arms. "I love you, baby. More than I will ever be able to tell you."

Another tight hug and he turned her loose. His voice choked around the words as he held back tears. "You need to get into the house. It's getting chilly out here." He motioned to the box of leftovers in the front seat. "Thanks for dinner and sending it home with me. I'll call and we'll see what we can do about next weekend."

Rayanne stood on the front porch and watched as the taillights disappeared. Hugging her arms around her she felt warm on the inside, but her father was right; it was cold out tonight.

The scent of dinner hung in the air mingled with the smell of happiness. Locking up, Rayanne was anxious to write to Luke. First a bath. She sprinkled bubble bath that Luke had bought for her in the tub and slipped into the warm fragrant water. Life felt perfect. It didn't seem possible how much it had changed since she opened the door to find Luke standing there less than a month earlier. She could stay in the bath for hours but as she relaxed her mind played over what she wanted to write in her letter.

The words flowed to the paper, as she sat at the table, still warm with a blanket wrapped around her shoulders.

Dear Luke,

Today has been perfect or it would have been if you had been here. I told you about my visit with my father yesterday. Today he brought my sewing machine over and stayed for dinner. I thought of you when I made a black berry pie. Your mother and Galen joined us and everyone liked what I cooked. We talked about you. Your mother misses you something fierce. I miss you too.

I forgot to tell you that they have set their wedding for Saturday after next. Galen told me tonight that he is surprising her with a trip to San Francisco.

This isn't as long as I thought it would be. I have so much to say to you but all of a sudden, I'm sleepy. I think it is because I took a long bath and used the bubble bath you gave me.

Write when you can and stay safe.
Rayanne

Rayanne yawned. She was having a hard time keeping her eyes open. She steamed the letter she had finished the night before open and slipped this one in behind it. Gluing it closed, she pressed her lips to the seal before she again set it by the door for mailing the next day.

****

Monday dawned bright and clear but fall was in the air. Rayanne loved the distinct aroma of this time of year. She wasn't quite sure what the scent was: ripe fruit ready for harvest, cool nights, leaves getting ready to turn, or a combination. Whatever it was, she wanted to open windows and doors and bring in as much of outside as she could to freshen the house.

By eleven o'clock the already clean house was sparkling and Rayanne sat down for a few minutes. It was almost a week since that fateful trip with Amber and Rayanne wanted, or more like needed to see and talk to her. She called her once, but long-distance cost money and they couldn't say much over the party line anyway. From living with Amber, Rayanne knew the schedule her friend kept, and even if Amber had to work tonight, she would be up by noon.

Rayanne drove toward Amber's feeling happy and blessed. Never could she have imagined finding the father she hadn't known she had. He'd been nothing more than a shadow in her life growing up. Fear of him kept her as silent as he had been. Neither of them had talked about her mother. What part had she played in their estrangement? Now, getting to know her father, she was sure her mother's bitterness had spilled over to Rayanne. They had agreed to let go of the past and move on from here, but it was a lot to get over, and yet, if she was going to have any good memories of her mother, she had to. As for her father, sadly it didn't appear that he had anything good to remember. Reflecting on all she had learned in the past two days pulled a shadow over the otherwise sunny day. Rayanne took a deep breath and vowed that she wasn't going to allow it.

By the time she pulled up in front of Amber's, Rayanne was back to a happy place. A place she needed to be for her friend. Not knowing what she was going to face, she knocked on the door, and waited. And waited. Darn, gas was at a premium with rationing. Plus, Rayanne wanted to start putting money aside for Luke when he came home, and she'd been running around too much.

Not wanting to waste the trip she sat down on the top step of the porch to wait. Betty, Ambers new roommate, worked the same shift so surely one of them would be home. Unless... Rayanne felt dread fill her. Could Amber have gone through with the abortion after all?

After almost an hour she decided to try the door again. This time when she knocked, she thought she heard movement inside. She knocked again and this time the door opened. Betty stood there looking like she'd just woke up.

"I'm sorry. I thought you and Amber would be up by now."

Betty opened the door wider in silent invitation to come in. "We should have been but it was a bad night." She turned toward the kitchen. "Come in. I'll put some coffee on."

Rayanne looked around the room. Everything looked in its place. "Is Amber still sleeping?"

"Amber is in the hospital."

Rayanne felt her heart drop. Her friend had gone ahead with the abortion, and if she was in the hospital, it was bad.

Betty motioned for Rayanne to sit down which she was thankful to do. "The coffee will be ready in a minute. We were walking home last night and Amber was complaining that her back was killing her. Thank heavens we were just a few houses down when she fell. Well, maybe more like collapsed. We managed to get her up and into the house but she was bleeding really hard. I wanted to call for an ambulance but Amber wouldn't let me. After almost an hour and the bleeding wasn't letting up, she finally agreed to a taxi."

"A miscarriage then?"

"No, well not really. It was a tubal pregnancy, but she's going to be all right."

Relief flooded through Rayanne. She was thankful that Amber hadn't gone ahead with the abortion. With the conditions she had described it probably would have killed her. "How long do they think she will be in the hospital?"

"That's the bad part. Of course, they had to do surgery which means four to five days in the hospital. Then maybe another six weeks off work. We are going to tell work it was an emergency appendectomy."

Reality settled over Rayanne. Knowing Amber, she didn't have any money saved. The phone company did have sick leave and Amber very rarely used any. Hopefully she had enough to get through this. It would have helped to have the money she'd given that doctor.

The scent of coffee filled the room and Rayanne was happy to have a cup. "I'll run over to the hospital."

"That would be swell."

****

Rayanne parked the car in the hospital lot and made her way into the reception area. Betty had stayed until after Amber's surgery the night before, but she was still in recovery when Betty had taken a taxi home so she didn't know the room Amber was in. Rayanne checked in and found out that Amber was in a ward on the maternity floor. As she walked down the hall, she could hear babies and mothers. Her heart fluttered to think that in a few months she would be in here with Luke's baby.

At the door she looked in. Four beds with curtains around them filled the room. Amber was in the last bed. She looked pale and, with no makeup on, younger.

"Hi," Rayanne whispered.

Amber pushed herself into more of a sitting position, cringing in obvious pain.

"Want me to raise the bed?"

"It doesn't work well. I'm okay. Thanks for coming. Did Betty phone you?"

"No, I decided to just drive in to see you. The last thing I expected was to find you in the hospital."

"I'll bet you're thinking all kinds of things."

Rayanne shook her head. "Betty told me. I'm so sorry, Amber."

"Don't be. The doctor said it will be harder to get pregnant with only one tube but I should be able to have children." She lowered her voice. "The girl over in the next bed had an abortion and almost died. As it is, she'll never be able to have kids. Makes me feel... I don't know. I guess humble?"

Rayanne was silent, digesting what Amber had told her. It could have been either of them. The war was taking an untold toll. Her heart hurt for those caught up in it.

Amber gave a sort of half laugh. "Makes one think of joining a nunnery."

"Sure, I can just see you," Rayanne quipped back.

The nurse came in and took Amber's temperature and blood pressure. "Looking good."

Amber nodded. Betty had sent some of Amber's toiletries with Rayanne. It would be nice to have her own stuff, especially her hairbrush.

"I feel so weak. And they want to keep me here for almost a week. Since I don't live alone, I'm going to try and talk the doctor into releasing me earlier."

"Okay, let me know and I'll come get you. Betty has to work so you can come stay with me."

"Do you mind? Maybe just until I don't get dizzy when I stand up."

"I don't mind a bit. I'll love having the company."

****

Amber worked her negotiating skills and was released on the third day. Rayanne got her settled and the next two weeks flew by. Luke's mother was like a hen with one chick. She made soup and baked goodies for Amber. That Amber didn't contact her own family didn't come up in conversation. Amber wasn't that close to her mother and younger sister. Staying with them was out of the question as far as Amber was concerned.

Luke's mother rapped on the kitchen door and walked in. Rayanne still forgot to lock the door during the day. She made a mental note to remind herself to say something when she left.

Amber who had bounced back to health, was

sitting at the kitchen table with Rayanne, being pretty verbal about the length of recovery time the doctor was imposing on her. "Really, I feel fine. It's not like I have a job where I need to be on my feet."

Luke's mom stayed long enough to soothe Amber reminding her she'd be back to work soon. When she left she flipped the lock on the door and smiled at Rayanne.

"You are so lucky, first Luke and then his mother love and take care of you." Ambers voice held a touch of wistfulness.

Rayanne sympathized with Amber, physically she looked pretty much recovered. But what about emotionally? They hadn't talked about the baby and maybe they should. Rayanne took a deep breath and sat down beside Amber. Starting with the obvious she said, "We haven't talked about the baby. How are you feeling about losing it?"

Her words seemed to echo in the room. Amber took her time and finally made eye contact with Rayanne. "You know, it's strange but the baby never seemed real to me. Maybe because it never could have developed into a child. I don't know, but I'm guessing it's not like having a miscarriage or even..." She paused and then said, "well, you know, what I was planning."

Silence filled the room.

Then a tear slid down Amber's cheek. "Oh Rayanne, I am so glad I didn't go through with it. That doctor, or whatever he was, saved me."

Rayanne reached over and squeezed Ambers hand. "I know," she whispered.

****

The next morning Amber got up early and even started breakfast for her and Rayanne. "Can you take me home today?" she asked as they washed dishes.

Rayanne agreed. She would drop Amber off and drive on out to her father's. He had called the night before and they had left today open.

Rayanne had continued her daily writing to Luke and as much as she hated to, told him Amber's story of the appendix. With Noah stationed in the same place Luke was, she didn't dare say anything about the pregnancy. Someday she would, when Luke was home.

The day went off as planned and Rayanne was happy as she drove home from her father's. Today she had found out that he had a terrific sense of humor and laughter filled the house and yard. She couldn't help think of how a child would add to the happiness. As if on cue she felt a flutter.

The baby had moved.

She slowed the car and put her hand over her tummy as an ache filled her heart. Luke should have been here to feel the first movement of his child.

It was dark when she got home and she went out to the mailbox before going in. An envelope lay in the box. Rayanne picked it up with shaking hands. A letter from Luke. *Finally.*

She hurried into the house and snapped on the living room light. Her heart was beating so hard she was surprised she couldn't hear it. The letter was dated almost two week earlier.

Dear Rayanne,
Mail is hard to get out right now. Sometimes it takes a while so not sure when you will get this. Even

though you might not hear from me, know that I am thinking of you... and the baby. And, that your letters bring light and hope from home.

I can't say where we are or anything about what's happening over here. Even if I did, it would be censored out. I know you are no doubt hearing horrible things, but the job I am doing is relatively safe and gives me renewed hope in the human spirit.

Noah is still with me and there is a side to him I hadn't seen stateside. He helps keep the guys' spirits up with his crazy humor. I wouldn't be surprised to see him go into the medical field when all this is over. For me, I will always want to be flying. I think maybe search and rescue. Commercial flying might get boring.

How is Amber doing? Has she already moved on with a new beau?

Can you maybe send me more pictures of you? I love the last one you sent. I carry it with me and tack it over head when I fly. Have I told you how beautiful you are? The guys tease me about having a pin-up wife. Pictures first, but the care package you sent couldn't have been better. I don't think it has stopped raining since we got here and I had forgotten what it felt like to have thick, dry wool socks. If you know of anyone who has guys over here, tell them socks are like gold.

I know this is short but lights are out and there is hardly any light to see by. Take care of yourself. And the baby. And, keep those letters coming.

Luke

Rayanne read the letter through three times before she put it down. A niggling worry penetrated her thoughts. She *hadn't* been following the news and what she had heard was that the allies were winning the war. Luke had warned her that war wasn't a game; that he had been prepared. And, he had assured her he was safe. She picked up the letter again and reread where he said "relatively safe." Shaking off the worry she thought about a picture she would send him. Maybe she'd have Gavin take one of her and his mother. She smoothed her skirt over her still small baby bump. Maybe if a breeze was just right the picture would show the baby.

Luke's image filled her senses, and with a smile she picked up her pen to start her nightly missive.

****

The weather had turned colder. Old folks predicted it would be a long hard winter and Rayanne didn't doubt that they were right. Especially when, on the night of Halloween, they had a spattering of freezing rain mixed with snow. The weather kept most people inside so there had been only a very few trick-or-treaters, and those had been out early. She would have left over candy, that was for sure.

Well maybe not. If they didn't come to her, she could always go to them. Rayanne put most of the candy in a sack and slipped into the new winter coat she had splurged on. A neighbor woman, June, had moved in a few weeks after Rayanne. Her husband had been overseas for over six months. The two women had hit it off and become instant best friends. Rayanne loved the two little kids: a girl aged five and a boy aged eight. June had brought them over earlier but with all the left-over treats, Rayanne decided to reverse trick-or-treat them.

Jimmy, the boy, answered the door with Dotty

right behind him. When they saw Rayanne they ran into her arms for a hug as she chimed, "Trick or Treat!"

Jimmy took her hand, ignoring the candy, and pulled her into the kitchen where his mother was finishing tidying up. Around her laughter, Rayanne managed another, "Trick or Treat," and handed them the sack of candy.

The kids joined in laughing.

"Oh, Aunt Ray, that's not the way you do it," Dotty lisped.

"It is when you have all this candy sitting around waiting for two little sweeties."

June wiped her hands and took down a couple of cups. "How about a cup of tea?"

Rayanne took off her coat and put it over one of the chairs. "Sounds good. It's horribly cold out there."

June agreed. "Makes for a quiet Halloween."

Rayanne stayed and helped June put the kids to bed. Then they settled back in the living room with another cup of tea. June's sigh filled the room. "I'm glad you came over. I miss Daniel so much. During the day with the kids, it's okay, but after they go to bed... well, you know."

Did she? Did she miss Luke like June missed her husband? They barely knew each other. And, yet those few mornings waking up next to him had been wonderful. The nights—Rayanne felt a blush creep up her face and ducked her head.

June sounded wistful. "Daniel is missing so much of the kid's growing up. They seem to change almost daily."

Rayanne thought about the little one due in a few months. What would Luke think about the changes in her? She'd sent him a picture but he hadn't commented on it. She doubted he would tack this one up in his plane. She for sure wasn't a pin-up girl anymore. Yearning filled her, would the war be over and Luke be back before his baby took its first steps? She pulled herself back from her musings. "Is Daniel career military?"

"No, like so many of our men he immediately enlisted after Pearl Harbor."

"What did he do in civilian life?"

"Daniel has his teaching credentials, but he was working in administration at the state. They will hold his job for him. Now all he needs to do is get back." June took a drink of her tea. "This really hits the spot on nights like tonight. Just not as good as a warm husband to curl up with." June laughed.

Both women reflected on June's words for a few minutes and then the conversation moved on to neighborhood gossip. True to what Galen had predicted the street of new houses filled up fast. The lots were pretty good sized so there were just fifteen houses. Rayanne and Luke's was the last house before the cul-de-sac with June's directly across the street. All the people on their street were around the same age with about half military. Rayanne felt more like part of a community every day.

June yawned and Rayanne glanced over. "Oh my gosh I hadn't noticed how late it was getting. I need to get home and let you get to bed. Dotty and Jimmy are going to be getting up before you know it."

"It isn't that late, and I loved having you over tonight. Still, there are mornings I envy you being able to sleep in a little."

"Yeah, and that will disappear in a few months when I age with sleep deprivation." Rayanne laughed.

They made plans for the next day and Rayanne let happiness flow through her as she made her way home. She hadn't seen Amber in a while and wasn't surprised as their lives had taken off in different directions. She sighed thinking of how friendships were so very subject to convenience, and renewed her thankfulness that she had connected with her father. Family was everything.

Letting herself into the silent house, melancholy filled with longing for Luke burned through her. She missed him more every day and even more at night.

Chapter 13

Luke stood just inside the barracks door, looking out. Would it ever quit raining? Between the rain and the humidity, nothing dried well. He had put on his last dry pair of socks that morning and hated the thought of sloshing through the wet to the mess house.

Noah came up behind him looking like he was in the same frame of mind. "Damn weather. And we thought Western Washington was bad."

"Did you get anything from Amber in yesterday's mail?" Luke asked.

"Are you kidding? I was surprised that she wrote a couple of weeks ago. I'm betting it is the last of her letters. Sounded to me like she is moving on."

Luke took a drag off his cigarette. He'd sworn them off, but had picked them back up over Christmas. "Yeah, from Rayanne's letters she isn't seeing much of her either. How do you feel about it?" Luke had been surprised to find that Noah was happy, more like thrilled, to get that letter a few weeks ago.

Noah shrugged. "It isn't like we had anything deep. Amber was out for a good time. And you know me."

Luke nodded. He did know Noah, or did he?

Noah changed the subject. "Think this will let up so we can fly?"

"Not today, but then you never know."

Both men fell silent as they reflected on Luke's

words. They were only two of three men trained to fly the helicopter's that took medical and essentials out to the soldiers in the field and brought in the wounded and dead. There was talk of more of the big birds coming in with personnel to fly them but so far it was only talk. Luke liked what he was doing. He loved flying, and the rescue side of it let him sleep at night. The few times he had flown a Spitfire and watched as his bullets brought down planes had left him with a sick feeling in his stomach and nightmares when he finally managed to sleep.

It was a no-mail call day so nothing to look forward to. Luke didn't want to add to the gloom. "Let's go see what's cooking over at the mess hall. Maybe someone has a book they are ready to loan out."

Noah laughed. "I'm on for chow but I don't know how you read so much."

"It brings new worlds to the now," Luke answered, thinking he didn't know what he'd do without books in his life. And, it was something that he had in common with Rayanne. They shared what they were reading and it brought him closer to her.

The day dragged on. Luke couldn't even get into the Ernest Hemingway novel, *For Whom The Bell Tolls*, he'd picked up. He finally gave up and closed his eyes. He would dream of Rayanne. He felt his body respond as thoughts of her filled his mind. It wasn't just the physical attraction—though that was over the top. He missed everything about her: her laugh, the way she treated her friends, even that stubborn streak of hers. When had his feelings changed? He silently chuckled. Had they changed? He wasn't sure he hadn't fallen in love that first night.

Luke bolted awake as the alarm signaling them to the command center sounded. The debriefing lasted a few minutes and they geared up to head out. It was a bad one with multiple wounded and a unit pinned down. The two helicopters were deployed out. Luke in one and Noah in the other.

It was almost an hour out to the unit that was under siege. Luke brought his bird down between the unit and enemy guns that bombarded them. Radioing Noah, he told him to set down on the other side of him so he would be a little more protected with Luke between him and the guns spitting death.

"What in the hell is going on here. Didn't they call for fighters? Fuck, Luke, we're a rescue unit, these birds don't have enough fire power."

"Their radio is out. I called back. We'll have help as soon as they can get in the air. Until then we'll do what we can."

"Not enough," Noah mumbled over the radio.

Luke unbuckled his harness and threw open the side door of the helicopter. "Damn!" What he was looking at was a scene out of hell. Air thick and caustic from weapons stung his throat and eyes. Men rushed out of the forest carrying and supporting wounded and started loading both the choppers. Luke could see the Nazi unit trying to set up a large mortar gun. That they hadn't had one was no doubt the reason the ground unit hadn't thought they needed fighters.

Luke's gaze swept over the terrain. Not good, his aircraft was sitting in between the Nazi gun and the American unit. Noah would likely get hit taking off and the exposed soldiers would be sitting ducks until they could get back into the trees.

They had loaded Luke with the more seriously wounded and, finished, the soldier gave Luke a thumbs up to take off. Luke looked over; the German gun was in position and waiting for a clear shot.

It took Luke only seconds to make the decision. Noah's helicopter was bigger than the one he had. It carried more cargo, but wasn't as fast or as maneuverable. Just as the door was closing, a man with blood running down his side slid through it. *What the hell. Abandoning his unit?* Though on second glance, Luke could see that he was barely able to walk. As he slid into the co-pilot's seat he said, "You need someone on the guns, sir."

"I need a lot more, at least someone in the rear."

"Yes sir, Adams has it covered. All he needed was someone to prop him up."

Luke's gaze locked with the other man's. "I hope you've brought a miracle aboard with you."

"Yes sir," the man responded.

Luke reached for the radio.

Noah had evaluated the situation himself. "They are going to shoot as soon as I clear the barrier you're making."

"I'm taking care of that. Lift off with me."

"As soon as they see what we're doing they will direct everything they have at us."

Luke couldn't wait another second. Looking over at his new co-pilot, and wishing with all his heart that it was only him on this bird, he spoke into the radio. "Go, and that's an order, Lieutenant." Thank heavens he outranked Noah—though just barely.

Luke watched as Noah started his lift off and rose into the sky with him. It wasn't only the two helicopters, the men still exposed in the field below would have the guns trained on them next. They would never get back to the protection the trees afforded. The gun or guns had to be taken out.

Lifting in unison, Luke gave one last look at Noah's loaded craft and turned back toward the enemy. The man in the seat next to him smiled and nodded. Then, with Luke putting the aircraft into a pattern it was never designed to do, the man opened fire with all he had blazing. Skimming over the Nazi guns Luke pulled another tricky maneuver that cleared them from the debris as the big gun blew to pieces.

"You did it, sir," the wounded man shouted.

Luke saw the soldier wipe blood from his mouth as his head lolled to one side. "We made it, soldier," Luke whispered.

In that instant the low hovering helicopter was rocked with bullets from the German soldiers. Sending a prayer of thanks when Luke saw the last of the ground soldiers make it back to the forest, he turned all his attention to getting his precious cargo home.

Luke felt a strange peace settle over him. The sounds from the wounded men seemed a long way off. Almost like they were coming from a tunnel. He shook his head trying to clear his vision. He didn't feel pain, just a numbing ache. How bad could it be? He felt along his upper leg and drawing his hand back saw it was covered in blood.

His blood.

The man in the co-pilot seat was unconscious.

Luke took a deep breath. He was going to bleed out if he didn't do something. Taking another deep breath, he unclasped his belt and drew it threw the loops.

Making a tourniquet, he drew it tight. He had to get this bird back to base.

Gritting his teeth, he set his mind to stay alert.

When the radio came alive with Noah's voice, Luke attempted to answer but couldn't budge his hands from the grip he had on the helicopter's controls. Almost at once he caught the other helicopter in his peripheral view. With a sigh he thankfully gave up trying to navigate and just followed.

****

Luke could smell the scent of hospital and hear the muted sounds around him. He wasn't in pain. Was he dead? A woman's voice finally emerged from the fog. "Lieutenant, can you hear me sir?"

Not Rayanne, she wouldn't call him Lieutenant. Luke fought to form an answer.

Then Noah's voice, so maybe he wasn't dead then. "Come on, you old sod. You've been asleep long enough."

Luke broke out of the fog as pain erupted through his body. "Damn, Noah, stop hollering." He groaned.

"Ah, there you are sir. Your buddy said he could wake you up." The nurse smiled at him.

"Been doing just that for most of this bloody war." Noah's voice still seemed to be booming.

"I didn't hurt until you penetrated whatever this nice fuzzy place is, you big goon," Luke croaked.

"Yeah, well someone had to do it."

The nurse put an end to their sparring. "You can come back after the doctor has seen him." With that she ushered Noah out and pulled a curtain around his bed. So, he was in a ward. That was a good thing; this wound couldn't be too serious.

Pain, like he'd never known before, radiated through his body. The doctor examined what felt like every part of him. By the time he left after a healthy dose of morphine, Luke was ready to drift back off to dream land.

****

Luke wasn't sure what day it was, only that weak sunshine shone through the hospital room. Slowly he took in the room around him. Noah was asleep in what looked like the most uncomfortable chair Luke had ever seen. Pain centered in his leg, and he cautiously looked down to make sure he still had it.

"What time is it?" he mumbled from a mouth that felt like he'd been in a desert dust storm.

Noah came awake with a jolt, and Luke smiled in satisfaction.

"Happy with yourself this morning, are you?" Noah groused.

Luke was, but more importantly he needed water and to pee. And, not in that order. "Buzz for a nurse," he mumbled.

Noah did better, he went out to find a nurse. Within a few minutes Luke was settled back in bed. Hurting, but at a tolerant level. When the nurse asked if he needed something for the pain, he shook his head. He wanted to hear how the mission had gone and how bad his own injuries were. For that he wanted a clear head. Almost immediately his thoughts went to Rayanne and his mother. Hopefully they hadn't been notified, because he could only guess at how that report would have gone. He needed to get a hold of them, to let them know he was all right. Hopefully, he was.

The nurse stuck a thermometer in his mouth,

effectively cutting off any questions. She applied a blood pressure cuff and pumped it up. "I know you have questions. The doctor will be here as soon as he can." Her tone was brisk, but her touch gentle.

As soon as the thermometer came out of his mouth, Luke didn't wait for the doctor. Some of his questions could be answered by the nurse or even Noah. "Where am I at?"

Noah took that question. "In London, with the next stop home, you lucky bastard." Glancing over at the nurse, he mumbled an apology.

"Go for it." She smiled as she left the bedside.

"London?" Luke liked the sound of that. "Did I crash, were the men with me—"

Noah didn't let him finish. "Never seen anything like that landing. You came in on a dime. Everyone that was alive when they loaded you, was still alive when you got them back."

"Even that gutsy guy that took over the co-pilot seat?"

Noah bobbed his head. "Jimmy McGregor, Irish through and through. He's been haunting this room in hopes of catching you awake."

Luke laughed. "Good. Swell."

A man with a stethoscope around his neck walked up to the bed and introduced himself as the surgeon who put Luke back in shape. "You had us worried for a while there. It seemed you lost more blood than most of us start out with."

Luke blew off the blood loss. He was more worried about his leg. "Did you manage to save my leg so that it will be as good as new?"

"We did, but again it was touch and go for the first

few days." The doctor looked down at the chart the nurse had been using. "I'm not going to sugar coat this Lieutenant, you're going to have to endure a lengthy rehabilitation to restore full use of that leg." He looked over at Noah. "No doubt your buddy here told you that this war is over for you."

Luke nodded. "How soon until I can be shipped stateside?"

"Ummm, depending on healing and transport logistics, maybe a couple of weeks." The doctor turned to go then stopped. "From what is coming in from the field, that was quite a rescue, with a hell of skilled flying. I'm more than happy that you're going to be fine and have no doubt you will ace whatever they throw at you in rehab."

Luke watched the doctor as he left. Laying back he thought about the hell he and the men had escaped from. Then almost immediately his thoughts turned to home. He was going home. He could almost smell the lilacs.

****

Rayanne opened the mailbox and let out a sigh. No mail from Luke. It wasn't all that unusual to go for a long spell without hearing from him, but for some reason this time she felt strangely uneasy. Last night she'd woken up to a horrible nightmare. Not that she could remember it, but the fear was still with her and her heart beat like crazy for a long time after she woke up. She pulled her coat tighter around her. Less than a month until spring but it looked and felt like winter had dug in. The sky had a gray cast and the air smelled like snow.

By the time she got back into the warm house,

Rayanne had decided to bundle up and walk down to Luke's mothers house. Galen would have left for work and Annie was always ready with a hot cup of coffee. Rayanne put on her boots. The road was icy and she was only a few weeks from having the baby. It wouldn't do to take a fall.

When Annie's house came into view Rayanne gave a sigh of relief. It had taken her longer than usual this morning. Rapping on the back door she opened it and hollered in. Annie was there in a flash. Worry was imposed on her face. "I'm so glad to see you. I was just getting my coat on to come down to your place."

Rayanne felt her heart leap until it felt like it was in her throat. Her first thought was "Luke." Something had happened.

Annie apparently could see the panic on Rayanne's face and quickly helped her off with her coat and told her to sit down. "I'm sure everything is okay. We got a letter from Luke. I just picked it up from the mailbox."

"You haven't read it?" Rayanne asked.

"It's addressed to both of us." Annie poured them both coffees as she talked. "It's his handwriting so he has to be okay."

Annie didn't sound as convinced as she was trying to be, and her hands were shaking so hard coffee sloshed over as she put a cup in front of Rayanne. Taking over, Rayanne wiped up the mess with a dishcloth and said, "Open it."

"Here, you read it." Annie held out the letter.

Rayanne took a deep breath and pulled the crisp paper from the envelope.

Dear Mom and Rayanne,

I'm all right, but I've been wounded. I know writing just one letter might not be the way to do this and I'll try to write to each of you later. As you can see, I am able to write even though it might be a little shaky. The good news is that I am expected to make a full recovery and that I still have all my pieces. But for me this war is over. The bad news is that I am going to need quite a bit of rehab to get my left leg working again. I hope you can put up with me. Noah says I'm a bear to get along with at the moment.

I'm not sure when I will be transported back to the States. The hospital here in London is a good one and they are taking great care of me. I know you must have a million questions and I'll answer them when I am back with you. For now, I seem to tire easily.

I can still receive those care packages you two send. I won't need any more wool socks so that will leave room for more brownies, candy, and cookies. Hint, hint.

See you soon. Take care of yourselves and the babe.

Sending love,
Luke.

Annie wiped at her eyes. "Oh my, I do have questions, but the main question he answered. He's going to be okay."

"I'm glad Noah is with him. Luke has never said much about Noah's family. I don't even know if he has any. Guess I'll keep sending Noah's packages with socks in them." Rayanne knew she was babbling on about something mundane, but she needed time to take in what Luke had written.

She drank the rest of her coffee and handed the letter to Annie. "I'm going to stop on my way home and let June know. I've been fretting so the last few days. It's like something was telling me Luke was in trouble."

Annie nodded. "You keep the letter."

"Okay. Thank you. But you can give it to me after Galen has a chance to read it."

The women hugged at the door. "Come down later," Rayanne said.

The air was still brisk and a wind had picked up. Rayanne knew she could have stayed, but she needed time to herself. Time to let it all sink in. To let her heart settle after hearing that Luke was hurt. And, to be happy that Luke was okay and coming home. The premonition of something wrong had caused almost a week of not sleeping well and she was worn out. Maybe she'd delay the visit with June until this afternoon.

Rayanne woke up from her nap feeling refreshed. And, energetic. Something that she had been missing this past week. Deciding to make a batch of cookies to take over to June's she headed for the kitchen. She no sooner pulled out her mixing bowl then the phone rang.

Picking it up, she was surprised to hear Amber's voice. They had let their friendship sort of fade since that fateful event in the fall. Rayanne had sent her a Christmas card but she hadn't heard anything back. Not that she was surprised. She would always think of Amber as a friend, especially since they had been through so much together, but she also knew friendships were dependent in large part to convenience. Some could keep going over a long distance but those were mostly friendships that spanned years. In the case of her friendship with Amber it hadn't been very long and they were so very different. Still, it was really nice to hear Amber's voice.

"Surprised?" Amber questioned.

"I am. It's been a while. How are you? Are you still working the swing shift?"

Amber's voice didn't hold a trace of humor as she said, "Whoa, it has been a while. Too long. I miss you. Can you come into town for a visit?"

Wow, Rayanne hadn't been expecting this. She looked outside and saw the sun shining; a perfect day to take a ride. She hesitated for a second. She wanted to go but should she with the baby's due date so near? Shaking off any worry she said, "I'd love to see you. Are you working today?"

"No, I actually have today and tomorrow off."

It was still early, not quite noon. "Then what about me coming in today?" Rayanne asked.

"Oh, I would love that."

A few minutes later, Rayanne had freshened up and was in the car. She stopped by Annie's to quickly run in and let her know where she was going. The baby was due in a couple of weeks and Annie worried so. Rayanne didn't mind; it felt good to have someone care about her.

As soon as Rayanne pulled the car over to the curb in front of Amber's place, she came out. She looked tired, but if she'd worked the night before and was coming off a week of working that wouldn't be unusual. Swing shift was hard though maybe not as bad as the graveyard shift Rayanne had been on.

Opening the passenger door Amber slid into the car. "I'm so glad you could come. I thought maybe we could get a bite to eat if that's okay?"

"Sure, that would be swell." Rayanne was glad she hadn't eaten lunch yet. "Where too?" she asked. Now that Amber was closer, Rayanne could see dark shadows under the other woman's eyes that even makeup wasn't hiding.

They decided on the little café that they used to go to in their old neighborhood. It held memories not only for them but of Noah and Luke who had joined them there.

Amber opened the conversation almost at once. "I got a letter from Noah." She waited for Rayanne to say something.

"Annie, Luke's mother and I got a letter this morning from Luke. He said the war was over for him and that he would be coming home. He made light of his injuries, but he did tell us it was going to take him time to get back on his feet." Rayanne paused, not sure she wanted to hear anything different. Finally, she asked, "What did Noah say?"

"Well, this is the first time he's written since he left so I was really surprised." She reached over and took Rayanne's hand.

Amber looked so serious. What was it? Was Luke critically hurt? Had he been glossing over his injuries? She swallowed the huge lump in her throat. Before she could say anything, Amber went on. "Noah was with Luke. Not in the same aircraft, but they had sent two helicopters in for a rescue. He said Luke is a hero and will no doubt get a medal. If he hadn't turned and attacked the Nazi gun none of them would have had a chance to get out. As it was, they got all the wounded out and covered for the ground unit to get back to cover."

Wow, Rayanne hadn't been expecting this. Her heart filled with pride. That along with love and relief that Luke was okay, surged through her. Everyday her love for him grew until it was going to be next to impossible for her to keep her promise to herself and him. A promise to not hold him to her but to let him move on with his life.

"I knew Luke probably wouldn't tell you everything." Amber smiled.

"No, he wouldn't."

"You've really fallen in love with him, haven't you?"

Rayanne took a sip of the tea the waitress had brought when she took their lunch order. "It shows, huh?"

Amber nodded, then changed the subject. "How was Christmas out in the boonies?"

"Boonies? Percy is a small town, but it is certainly not in the boonies. In fact, it's a lot closer to the base than here."

The waitress came with their sandwiches and both women found they were hungry. Rayanne filled Amber in on her holidays, which were the best she could remember. She told Amber about reconnecting with her father. Amber had been mostly quiet and now Rayanne turned the conversation back to her. "What about you? You look tired?"

"Me? Oh, you know, fun and games. Between play and work, it wears a girl out."

Rayanne wasn't going to let Amber off the hook. "It looks like more. How's work?"

"The same. Betty is getting married," Amber blurted out.

"And you're worried about getting another roommate?" Rayanne prompted.

"I wish. You know the place we have was Betty's and I moved in with her. The guy she is marrying is a soldier and is being deployed." She stopped for a second. Then said, "Sound familiar?"

Rayanne nodded. "Yeah, sort of but won't that work out better for you?"

"It would, but Henry, her fiancé, doesn't like me and he wants his sister to stay with Betty while he's overseas. Plus, not liking me, Henry thinks I'm a bad influence on Betty." Amber looked down at her hands where they rested in her lap. "Ha, I'd say that went both ways. Betty likes a good time as much or maybe even more than I do. Henry is so strait-laced that I can only imagine what her life is going to be like. Though it's mine I'm worried about right now."

"Of course. I can understand. Will Betty be quitting her job?"

"She wouldn't need to," Amber said, "and I don't think she wants to, but Henry is insisting."

"Wow, I'm feeling sorrier for Betty every minute."

Amber chuckled. "Now that you say it, I think I am too."

Rayanne finished her sandwich. "I could use a refill on this tea. How about you?"

"I don't have to be anywhere but I should pick up a paper and look for places to rent." She shrugged her shoulders. "What the heck, that can wait. It feels so good to be able to talk this through. You always help me put things in perspective."

The waitress came over with more tea and Rayanne waited for her to leave before continuing their conversation. "If the phone company hires someone new, maybe they will need a roommate. Until something comes up, Betty's apartment has two bedrooms so to heck with this Henry. He can just simmer down and give you time to find something."

Amber took a drink of her tea and fell silent for a second. Then said, "The only problem is that Henry isn't being deployed for another month so he will be moving in this coming weekend. You can imagine how uncomfortable that is going to be."

"Gosh, Amber, I'd love to have you stay with me but it's so far from the phone company. My gas rations would never stretch to drive you back and forth."

"Thank you. I know you would if you could." Typical of Amber, she seemed to recover and even sounded cheery. "Let's pick up a newspaper and take it back to the apartment. Betty already gave up her job so she will be there, but Henry won't come over until later when he gets off work at the base."

Chapter 14

Betty was in her bedroom when Rayanne and Amber got back. Amber cleared off a spot on the kitchen table and they opened the paper to the ads. "Actually, there are quite a few places. More than I thought there would be," Amber said.

"That's good." Rayanne glanced up to see Betty leaning against the door frame.

"You don't have to worry about moving out." Betty came further into the room and it was apparent that she'd been crying even though it looked like she had tried to hide it with makeup.

Amber still had her head down looking at the paper and didn't see what Rayanne did. She nudged her foot with Ambers to get her attention.

"What?" Amber mumbled.

Rayanne ignored her and asked Betty if she wanted her to make a pot of coffee.

"I can do it." Betty shuffled over the coffee pot. Shaking the pot, she said, "Actually I'll just warm this up."

Amber looked up. The shock on her face at seeing what Betty looked like echoed Rayanne's reaction.

Betty sat down. Closer now, she looked even worse. Not only was her face blotchy from crying, there was a long cut on her cheek that ran down to her jaw. "I know. I look horrible."

"No," Amber quickly said.

"Come on, you are a terrible liar."

"What happened?" Rayanne asked.

"Henry." Betty didn't get further before she burst out in tears.

Amber handed her a napkin. "Did he hit you?"

Betty nodded.

"Has he hit you before?" Rayanne asked.

"Not like this." Betty got up and poured coffee. With her back turned, Rayanne and Amber had to strain to hear her.

Amber got up and took the coffee pot from her. "Here, let me do this. You sit down and tell us what's going on."

Betty blew her nose. "First, you don't have to move out. There isn't going to be a wedding."

"Did you tell Henry? Is that why he hit you." Amber pushed a cup over to Betty.

"No, I haven't told him yet." Betty sighed. After a few seconds she continued in a monotone voice. "He... Henry wanted to... you know, this morning."

Amber and Rayanne both nodded their heads but didn't say the "sex" word.

"I said no, it was the wrong time of month. And he knew that from last night already. He got mad and called me a few names, then stomped off to the bathroom." She looked over at Amber. "I'm surprised that he didn't wake you up with all the slamming around."

Amber shook her head.

"Anyway, I went out to make him some breakfast. He took one bite of his eggs and started cursing. He threw the plate at me and it broke." She pointed to her chin. "I can't marry him," she whispered.

"No, of course not," Amber answered.

"Henry wanted to go to the bank with me this afternoon and put his name on my bank accounts so they will be joint. I've been saving money. Not a lot but enough to get by for a little while."

Amber shook her head. "You're lucky you didn't get that far. And maybe you can get your job at the phone company back?"

"I was worried about having a mutual account with him. But the wedding is a week from Friday. I knew I'd need to combine things. It isn't as if he doesn't contribute. We were going to take care of as much as possible this afternoon."

Amber reached over and took Betty's hand. "I don't think you should be here by yourself when you tell him."

Rayanne agreed. "He might be dangerous. I'll stay too."

"Oh, no. You are pregnant and if things do turn bad, I don't want you to get hurt. I've thought this out and while you were gone, I called a lock smith to change the lock on the door." She glanced at the wall clock. "He should be here any minute. I'm thinking of locking the doors and leaving. Henry won't be able to get in with his key. That will be his first clue."

Rayanne was impressed with how brave Betty was. She wasn't sure she would be. Rayanne said as much, then said, "You are still going to have to face him. Let us stay and maybe pack up the stuff he has here. That way after you tell him, he won't have a reason to come back."

Betty nodded. "I'm glad he's going to be deployed.

If I can get through the next three to four weeks he will be out of country." She started sobbing again.

Rayanne stood and put her arm around Betty's shaking shoulders. Looking over at Amber she could see that they shared the same thoughts. This wasn't going to be an easy breakup, and they couldn't leave their friend to do this on her own.

With all three women working together it wasn't any time before they had Henry's things boxed up. Betty looked at the pile. "I don't think I want to let Henry in. We can shove these boxes out in the hall. I can say everything I need to through the door." Betty turned her engagement ring around on her finger. "Except for this. I need to hand it to him."

"I can stay until after you talk to him and then you and Amber should come home with me," Rayanne offered.

Amber thought that was a good idea. "That way you can lock up the apartment and won't have to worry about him trying to get in."

They had no sooner decided on the plan and got the stuff out in the hall then they heard the outer door open. *Henry!* Rayanne's heart was in her throat as they waited for him to reach the door and see the boxes.

They heard him before he came all the way down the hall. "What the hell is all of this?" He tried the door and found it locked. Knocking, or more like hammering, on the door, he bellowed Betty's name.

"Let him try his key," Amber whispered.

The women listened to Henry cursing loudly and calling Betty names.

Betty's face was white. "I'm so glad you are both here. I'm scared to open the door to give him the ring."

Rayanne held out her hand. "Let me have the ring. You go in and call the police."

"Aren't you scared?" Amber whispered.

Rayanne nodded. "Petrified, but I doubt if he will hit a woman so pregnant."

"I'm not sure," Betty whispered.

The phone was on a wall in the kitchen. Rayanne pointed toward it. "Call the police and tell them to hurry. I'll try to talk to him through the door. With any luck they will get here and you can give them the ring to return to him."

Betty hurried off to phone, but Amber stayed with Rayanne. "I wish we'd called the police earlier."

"I do too." The noise of Henry trying to force the lock stopped and both women held their breaths. Rayanne gripped the ring in her hand, hoping that the police would be quick.

Henry's voice quieted. "Come on, honey. If this is about what happened at breakfast, I'm sorry."

Rayanne held her breath as Henry continued to plead. It made her stomach turn. She was so lucky to have Luke. He'd never shown her anything but gentle kindness. He wouldn't like that she was in this situation. Rayanne looked over at Amber. "Do you think I should try to talk to him? To maybe give him the ring?"

The lock smith had put a sturdy chain on the door. Amber said, "I don't know. If you open the door, he might break the chain and force his way in."

"Go see if Betty got a hold of the police and if they are on the way."

Henry was back to shouting curse words.

Betty came in from the kitchen and stepped up to

the door. "The police are on their way," she whispered. Then in a louder voice said, "Stop it, Henry. I've called the police. When they get here, I'll give you your ring back. We're over."

"Aw, come on honey. I didn't hurt you. The wedding is all set for this Saturday. What will your friends and family say?"

Betty looked at Rayanne and Amber and whispered, "More like what will his mother and sister say when they find out they aren't taking over my apartment." She raised her voice. "I think they will be happy for me. Mom tried to warn me."

"Your mom is an old bitch."

"Boy, way to win you back." Amber kept her voice low.

The words were no more than out of her mouth when they heard the siren. A few minutes later and they could hear Henry talking to the patrol officer.

"I want this all finished and it won't be until I give him back this ring." Betty unlocked the door but kept the chain on. When she saw two uniformed policemen she said, "Officer, could you give him back this ring?" She held it up to the crack in the door.

"Yes ma'am." He took the ring and held it out to Henry. "You need to go. If we get another call, we will have take you into the station."

Rayanne knew Henry was no fool. The military didn't take well to being called by the local police. With the war he probably wouldn't be discharged, but he'd no doubt be confined to base and maybe lose rank.

The women watched from the crack in the door. With the officers between Henry and the door he didn't say another word. Picking up one of the boxes, the officer picked up the other one. "Thanks," he mumbled and without a backward glance he left.

Betty opened the door to the remaining officer. "Thank you."

He took a look at her bruised face and nodded. "I doubt he'll bother you again. We know what he is driving and will keep an eye out, though."

Again, Betty thanked him and with a sigh of relief closed the door and sat down on the sofa. "I should have done something way before this. He's been verbally abusive before but never physically."

Rayanne sat down beside her. "It's over. Think what your life would be like if you'd married him?"

Betty shuddered. "Horrible." She smiled and turned to Amber. "So, you don't need to find another place."

"Swell." Amber laughed. "Though I think I have a few gray hairs from this afternoon."

Betty smiled at Rayanne. "Thank you. And, thanks for the offer of going home with you, but I need to stay and start canceling all the wedding stuff. It wasn't going to be very big so at least we won't need to notify too many people."

Rayanne understood.

"I'll stay and help her," Amber offered.

By the time Rayanne got home her ankles were swollen and she was thankful to put them up on the sofa. She'd gotten the mail from the box on her way in and opened a letter from Luke. Her heart sped up as she again thought of her handsome husband. His opening words almost jumped off the paper.

My darling wife,
There I've said it. I know we decided this was only

a temporary marriage, but over the past months I've gotten to know you and I want more. Though I do understand if you don't want to go through the process of rehab with me. I know it isn't going to be a picnic. At least it looks like I'll keep the leg. For a while there, I was sure I would lose it, and if that would have happened, I wouldn't have wanted you to try and make our marriage real.

Rayanne stopped reading and wiped her eyes. Did he really think so little of her? Her thoughts went to Betty and Henry. How different her life was than Betty's or Amber's. And, what about Noah? They had all loved him and yet Amber had never depended on him. Not even to tell him she was pregnant.

She picked the letter back up.

I hesitate to write this when I yearn to tell you in person. That's not all I yearn for either. Anyway, here it goes. I love you and I'm in love with you. As I've gotten to know you, I've seen how truly beautiful you are. Certainly, I could see that, but you are beautiful inside as well. My mother feels like she's gained a daughter and for that I am truly thankful.

They are starting to turn the lights out. I hope I haven't scared you. I know I should wait, but I had to tell you how I feel.

I'll be home soon.

Love you.

Luke

Rayanne sat back and closed her eyes as Luke's words filled her.

After a short rest she picked up her pen and started writing back to Luke. In the beginning of Luke's deployment, she had written something every day. At first it was only a few sentences and it would sometimes take a week to make it a letter worth the postage to send. Gradually her nightly missive had grown until now she shared her inner thoughts. Luke wrote more too and she grew to know him as a little boy, a young man, a pilot, and a soldier. The more she got to really know him, the more she fell in love. Now, she started the letter with a shortened version of what had happened at Betty's and Amber's.

After a short break to use the bathroom Rayanne made a cup of tea and again picked up her pen.

How do I tell you what is in my heart? I feel like I am the luckiest woman alive to have the love of a man like you. Like you, through our letters, I've gotten to know you. I can't help but wonder if we would have ever really had this if miles hadn't separated us.

Oops, baby just got in on this conversation with a strong kick. She: did I tell you I am almost certain we have a girl? I hope you won't be disappointed. We need to start thinking of names. It won't be long before she meets the world. I was thinking of Lucia Rayanne. Lucia for you and your dad, Ray for my Dad, Anne for your mother and Rayanne for me.

I want to get this in tomorrow mornings mail so I need to close. I can't wait for you to be home. I can't wait to be with you, going to bed at night and waking up with you in the morning.

Love you to the moon and back.

Your wife.

Rayanne clumsily got off the couch. It took her longer these days. She was glad she was on her feet when there was a knock on the front door. It wasn't late, just barely dark. Thinking it was either June from next door, or Anne, she hurried to answer it.

The light from the living room shone on the porch of a tall man in uniform. "Ma'am, we have a delivery for you." He looked tough, and then he smiled and stepped to the side.

Luke sat in a wheelchair that a second man had pushed him to the porch in. He started to stand but before he could, Rayanne had flown out the door and was almost in his lap.

"Whoa, think she's glad to see him?" the man that had knocked on the door said.

Laughter erupted from all four of them.

"Sorry for the time but the Captain here wanted to wait until night set in so it would be easier to surprise you."

"This hero stuff gets a little much," Luke mumbled. Then, having none of being wheeled into his home, he asked for the crutches. The two men stood back as he slowly got to his feet and made his way inside. He stopped and looked around at the home Rayanne had made. Bright pillows made the couch look inviting. "I like what you've done."

This was the first time he had gotten a good look at her and Rayanne felt herself flush as his gaze took in her body. The house wasn't the only thing changed.

"My god, you are beautiful."

All of sudden it didn't matter that her feet were swollen or that she could compete with an elephant. She felt beautiful.

"Need us for anything more, sir?" the military guy asked.

"I can handle it from here. Thanks for the help."

Both the men stepped forward and saluted Luke.

"Anytime sir. It's an honor."

The wheelchair was brought inside and in seconds the house fell quiet. Luke almost fell on the couch. "You may have to help me up." His voice sounded gruff.

"Gladly," she said.

Rayanne thought of the letter she had just received and the one she had just finished writing. Luke didn't know she had received it and would be wondering where they went from here. Maybe he even thought she didn't want him home. Nothing could be further off.

She sat down next to him and then got up on her knees to reach him better. Taking his face in her hands she whispered. "I am so glad you're home." She paused and then said, "I love you. I love you more than I can ever tell you."

"You got my letter?"

Rayanne nodded. "I got it in today's mail." She paused and watched as what she was feeling was reflected in Luke's eyes. "I already wrote you back," she whispered.

"Let me read it."

She slowly got off the couch and retrieved the still open pages before laying them in his lap. Luke's eyes misted as he read her letter while Rayanne sat quietly beside him.

Afterward he took a bit to find his voice. "I love her name."

"Oh, Luke." Rayanne bent over and touched her lips to his. That was all it took for Luke to pull her into his lap.

"You'll hurt yourself," Rayanne whispered.

Luke's gaze moved over her. "Worth it," he mumbled as he covered her lips with his.

Epilogue

Rayanne hummed as she made breakfast. Little two-month-old Lucia was sleeping soundly, so the morning, at least for the moment, was hers.

"Happy wife." Luke smiling, came into the kitchen. Pulling her into his arms he gave Rayanne a hearty good morning kiss.

"Umm," she mumbled, returning the kiss.

Luke pulled her tighter against him letting her know what he was feeling. Laughing she turned off the stove. They didn't even try to deny how they felt about each other.

Both sated they quietly lay beside each other.

"Is it always going to be like this?" Rayanne asked as she cuddled closer.

"I sincerely hope so."

With a sigh, she sat up. "I need to get you some breakfast before the little princess wakes up and wants hers."

"Lay here with me for a bit. If she wakes up, I'll make you breakfast," Luke replied. He was getting around better every day and except for when they had a lot of walking to do, he didn't use the wheelchair. "I've been thinking about going back to work."

Rayanne moved so she could see him. "Flying?" She loved having Luke home. He was the essence that she hadn't known she was missing.

"Maybe not flying, at least not for a while. I thought I'd talk to the Commander after I get through with therapy today. See what he thinks."

Rayanne didn't say anything. She didn't think there was anything she could say to change his mind. Luke was his own man, and she knew he hated that he wasn't a hundred percent.

He reached over and gave her a light kiss. "Honey, we need to get our lives back to normal."

"I know, but Lucia and I love having you with us."

Luke laughed and the sound filled the room. "You do a man's ego a lot of good. I was afraid you'd get tired of me limping along."

"Not on your life."

A happy baby gurgling sound came in unison with a knock on the front door. "Ah, I think Grandma has a built-in alarm that's set to Lucia time."

Luke let out a mock sigh. "Can't wait until tonight. Bedtime seems to come later and later."

Laughing Rayanne quickly pulled on her robe and went to let Annie in. Luke got dressed and headed for the baby's room.

Spring sunshine brightened the house depicting her life. Rayanne's heart filled with joy. When she opened the door the scent of lilacs filled the air. The scent of home. The scent of love.

About the Author…

Lavada lives in the beautiful Pacific Northwest. She is an avid reader, enjoying almost all genres. She takes the advice to write what you enjoy reading to heart and her goal is to write books that cross genres, taking the reader on different paths with equally enjoyable and captivating stories.

A dreamer, Lavada has a need to create. She worked in the computer field designing and developing first mainframe applications and later web sites. The art of writing has proved to be a challenge but it gives her satisfaction beyond anything she could have dreamed.

Lavadadee.com

Thank you for purchasing
this publication of The Wild Rose Press, Inc.

For questions or more information
contact us at
info@thewildrosepress.com.

The Wild Rose Press, Inc.
www.thewildrosepress.com